RUPERTA

erta and her father, Prince Rupert, were
ed to the continent following the defeat
Charles I, returning to England after the
storation. As she grew up, Ruperta was
ious to find the mother she had never
own, but her journey to her mother's old
me was interrupted by a highwayman,
to stole her possessions but allowed her to
cape with her life. Finding shelter with
remy and Ann Colston, she is introduced
to their neighbour, the handsome Roger
udworth, who seems strangely familiar.
oon, she is plunged into mystery and
itrigue – and finds herself in jail.

RUPERTA

Ruperta

by

Lloyd Peters

Dales Large Print Books
Long Preston, North Yorkshire,
BD23 4ND, England.

British Library Cataloguing in Publication Data.

Peters, Lloyd
    Ruperta.

    A catalogue record of this book is
    available from the British Library

    ISBN   978-1-84262-527-9 pbk

First published in Great Britain by IPC Magazines Ltd. 1982

Copyright © IPC Magazines Ltd. 1982

Cover illustration © Nigel Chamberlain by arrangement with
Alison Eldred

The moral right of the author has been asserted

Published in Large Print 2007 by arrangement with
Lloyd Peters

Dales Large Print is an imprint of Library Magna Books Ltd.

Printed and bound in Great Britain by
T.J. (International) Ltd., Cornwall, PL28 8RW

CHAPTER ONE

Ruperta gazed into the gathering dusk and wondered how long it would be before she reached Chodbury. The subdued sounds of hoof beats and the wind penetrated the coach, and the rise and fall of the wheels on the uneven ground jerked her head in short, restless movements against the seat back.

She glanced at her two male travelling companions who sat opposite each other. A clergyman, a tall man huddled into his enveloping cloak, eyes closed. Was he planning a sermon? The other sat upright, his gaze fixed.

She drew her hood forward, snuggled into her cloak. It was getting cool, the evening bringing with it the promise of frost to come in the not too distant future. She was weary now, having left London the day before, stopping overnight at Kinnerton and now approaching the end of her journey.

Had she been foolish coming so far by herself to search for someone she might never find? If her father had known what she was doing, he would very likely have packed her off to France.

Here she was, the daughter of Prince Rupert, having set out to try and find the mother whom she had never known. Many were the times she had asked about her, but the Prince had always changed the subject, been evasive. As Ruperta had grown older, the feeling that she must find out who her mother was had grown stronger.

Her father had never married, and Ruperta guessed that he had felt deeply about her mother. She had seen the momentary change in expression in his eyes whenever she had broached the subject. Ruperta felt that he had loved the woman who had borne his child.

Ruperta had decided that at the first opportunity she would seek out her mother. Just to see her. Perhaps not even to speak with her. Then she would have satisfied the curiosity that had brought her so far from home.

It had not been easy either to find the opportunity or to gather such information as she could regarding her mother's name, and the whereabouts of the house where she – Ruperta – had been born. For one thing, her apartment was quite close to her father's in London, and although she did not see him very often, he was apt to visit her without warning.

Throughout her young life she had seen very little of him, but during their long exile on the Continent after the defeat and execution of her great-uncle, Charles I, her father had seen to it that she had been well educated and looked after. Then, after the Restoration, she and her father had returned to England, an England she knew nothing of, having been too young to remember anything about it.

Her opportunity came some five years later when the Prince told her that he would soon be with the Fleet, and did not expect to return for some time. She had decided there and then to begin her search for her mother when her father was gone.

By dint of patient and discreet inquiry from older servants and her duenna, she found out that the midwife who had delivered her was still alive. Ruperta went to see her, and found her very unwilling to speak out. The old woman protested that she must keep the secret. She might lose the roof over her head if she uttered one word upon the matter. Prince Rupert was a man to be obeyed, she said.

But Ruperta had pleaded, vowing that she herself could be trusted to keep quiet about the source of the information she wanted.

After much deliberation and sighing the old woman told her: 'The house you want is Ravall's Court, Chodbury.'

And now Ruperta was approaching Chodbury in the dusk of an autumn evening twenty-one years after leaving the district as a very young child…

Suddenly she was aware of the coach swaying and shaking, of shouts. She glimpsed a horseman galloping alongside, and held on to her seat to stop herself being thrown to the floor. Both her companions were now looking thoroughly alarmed as they, too, clung on.

The figure on horseback was near enough for her to see him brandishing something. What was happening? The swaying had increased. She and the others were being tossed about. Then there was a savage jolt, and the carriage went down at Ruperta's side. She gave an involuntary cry of fear. Her head hit the side of the carriage, and her companions fell on the floor in an undignified heap. There was a tearing, scraping sound and the coach came to rest, canted heavily to one side.

A momentary silence, then raised voices outside. Shocked, Ruperta remained where she was, still clinging on. Everything had happened so quickly. Ruperta's companions began to clamber to their feet. One of them opened the carriage door. Then he turned to Ruperta. 'You are not hurt?' he said.

She shook her head, gave a weak smile. Cold evening air filled the carriage.

'I'll wager it's a broken wheel,' said the second of her companions.

A voice came from outside, impatient mockery in it. 'Thought to outrun me, did you? It'll take more than those nags and a coach to get away from me.'

Ruperta heard a horse move. The voice came again, nearer.

'Jolting poor passengers like that renders them in no fit state to receive me.' A chuckle. 'I like to do this business pleasantly, without ill-feeling if possible.' The tone sharpened threateningly. 'So sit still up there, don't move. I don't want to have occasion to use my pistol, but I will, if you give me cause.'

Ruperta peered round the carriage door. Horse and rider were darkly outlined against the sky. She withdrew quickly, pressing herself as far back into the corner of the carriage as she could. Her mouth was dry, her heart

11

beating wildly. The tales she had heard, the stories about such happenings as this had always seemed unbelievable to her. But this moment was horribly real. A highwayman had stopped the coach.

'Come along, gentlemen, step outside, please. Divest yourselves of your valuables. Have a care in handing them over – make sure you keep nothing back.'

Ruperta looked on as her two companions descended with some difficulty from the coach, the clergyman being first out.

'Ah, a man of the Church!' the highwayman exclaimed.

'You would rob one of my calling?' said the clergyman.

'It touches my conscience not a bit. Some of this you give me came, no doubt, from some poor wretch ill able to afford it,' said the highwayman. 'And now, get out of the way. There are others waiting to give.'

'I shall make it my business to see you hanged for this,' Ruperta's other companion said harshly. 'I am a magistrate.'

Ruperta heard the tinkling of coins, and wondered anxiously if the highwayman had seen her. If he had, he was not going to bother with her yet.

He said thoughtfully: 'The Church and

the Law! Both excel at taking from others. No matter, you should be able to make it a worthwhile night for me.'

'I'll give you nothing, you rogue,' the magistrate snapped.

Ruperta heard the click of metal. 'Be careful of your words,' the highwayman said. 'You show no mercy to some of those before you. And there will be none for you unless you hand over everything in the way of money and valuables you have on you.'

Grunts of anger, mutterings followed. The highwayman spoke again. 'It has pleased me greatly to relieve you of this. No doubt you sat under Cromwell and helped to bankrupt the Royalists. Well, I and others do not forget. Stand away before my anger makes me pull this trigger.' The voice was charged with suppressed emotion.

'I'll see you swing in chains on Shorrocks Moor for this,' said the magistrate with savage intensity.

'Perhaps you will.' The highwayman's tone was calmer now. 'But not before I've redressed the balance somewhat – collected a lot more from men like you.'

Then Ruperta heard the voice of the clergyman. 'Repent now while there is time. Otherwise it will be the worse for you.'

The highwayman laughed scornfully. 'Will the Church feed me, pay me, recompense me?'

There was a momentary silence, then a creak of harness, a movement of the highwayman's horse. 'Was it a woman I saw peering out a while back? A pretty one, too, if I'm not mistaken.'

His voice startled Ruperta, sounding just outside the carriage. She edged forward on her seat to look up at him. A mask hid most of his face, but his mouth smiled down at her. The horse snorted and shook its head.

'Ah, my first notion was correct; you are pretty. Nay, more than that.' He sighed. 'Pity I have not the time to go into the question. It is against my principles to take from a lady, but as you see I must treat all of you alike, otherwise these gentlemen would complain. So I must ask you to give me your money and any trinkets you carry.' His voice had lost its roughness.

But Ruperta was in no state to notice that. She was upset, shocked. If she gave him all the money she had with her, she would be stuck in the middle of the English countryside without means of getting back to London. The prospect was frightening, perhaps even more so than the man demanding money from her.

'You will hasten, please. I have not much time.' There was a slight hardening of the voice.

With a sigh of despair Ruperta undid the purse corded to her wrist. He reached down for it. 'Perhaps you have some jewellery or some more money?'

It must be a dream, she thought. She would soon wake up.

'Please.' The tone was sharp – brooked no defiance.

She fumbled at the pocket inside her cloak, unable to believe what was happening to her. Grasped the large coins. Left one. The metal clinked into his palm.

'Now, show me both hands, please,' he ordered.

Even in the poor light the pearl on her finger glowed like a young moon. 'Please! Don't take that,' she pleaded. 'It was given to me by my father.'

The pearl itself had been part of a collection belonging to Elizabeth of Bohemia, her father's mother. He had had it set in a ring for Ruperta. She hesitated. 'You have my money. Will you not leave me this – this gift from my father?'

'Oh, would I not prefer a man to rob!

15

Women pull at the heartstrings too much,' he said with irritation. 'It seems to me that it holds more value than the coins you have given me. That is, if it is real.' He gave the slightest of bows. 'And judging by many things about you, I think it must be.' He glanced about him quickly. 'So please! I cannot linger over this transaction any longer.' He held out his hand again.

Miserably, Ruperta began to slide the ring from her finger. She was cold, her head was hurting where she had banged it against the side of the coach, and she regretted bitterly that she had ever set out on the journey. A foolish, madcap one it appeared now! Reluctantly she placed the ring in the hand extended to receive it.

Perhaps it was the sight of his fingers closing over her treasured possession that sparked the fury that suddenly erupted in Ruperta. She clung to the carriage door, half in, half out of it. 'You despicable rogue! You rob a defenceless woman of her most treasured possession. D'you want the clothes off my back also? Only a craven, cowardly thief would leave me here, penniless, a prey to other wolves like yourself. Is your need so great that you have to steal? It will not be on your conscience that your actions nearly wrecked the coach and hurt my head. Leave us, count your money. I hope you will not live long to enjoy it. Wherever this moor is, I hope they do hang you on it.'

There was a silence after her outburst, broken only by the wind rustling the leaves on the near-by trees. She could not see what effect her words had had on him. The mask and the poor light hid his expression. In any case she was past caring, and slumped back into the carriage seat in numbed hopelessness. What was she going to do, stuck in a broken-down coach with no money, no valuables to sell? Never in her life had she felt so helpless. And with a new fear beginning to penetrate her mind. Soon it would be dark and she would be alone with these men.

'Step down from the coach, my lady,' the highwayman told her.

Stiffly and somewhat awkwardly Ruperta clambered down to stand looking up at him in great apprehension. Had she gone too far? Yet there had been neither threat nor malice in his voice.

He waved his pistol in the direction of the others. 'Cut one of the horses free. Bring it here and quickly,' he ordered. He looked down at Ruperta. 'Does your head still pain you?'

'Yes, it does,' she snapped.

The horse was brought to where she stood.

'Now get up on it,' the masked man ordered.

She stared up at him in amazement. 'B-but – w-what are...' she stammered.

'Get up on the horse,' he said curtly.

Ruperta looked at the animal. No saddle – but the horse did have a bit, and the highwayman was busy with what would serve as a leading-rein.

He spoke harshly over her head. 'Hey, man of the Church. Give the lady a hand up. And no tricks, or there'll be one fewer of your calling.'

Moments later Ruperta clung to the animal, her mind still in a whirl. She looked at the group of men by the coach in the gathering darkness.

The highwayman said to them: 'It is only about ten miles to Chodbury. The sooner you start, the sooner you will be there.'

With that he wheeled his mount, grasping the leading-rein of Ruperta's horse, and they moved off. Shouts of rage followed them.

Ruperta was bewildered and afraid. What was going to happen to her now? What did the highwayman intend to do with her – hold her to ransom? She discarded the idea almost immediately. It was highly unlikely that he knew who she was. No one had known that she was going to travel at that particular time, and she was not well known outside London, or in it for that matter. She had used another name during the overnight stop in Kinnerton...

After some minutes the man slowed his horse, and she cast a glance at him. He had said nothing since leaving the others. She could not see his face, darkness was falling; he was only a shape against the sky.

'W-where are you taking me?' she said at last.

'You will see,' he replied curtly.

Anger, partly born of fear and partly of dislike, flared in her again. 'You have no right to detain me like this! I demand that you take me back. You have my money, and my ring. What more do you want?'

'I want nothing more from you, Mistress Spitfire. I have cause to thank you this night.'

'And well you might, the amount you have robbed me of!'

He ignored that and said: 'I am about to do you a favour.'

'Oh.' What was he talking about?

'I am taking you to a place where you will get food and drink, warmth and shelter for the night.'

'But where…' she began.

'No more questions!' he interrupted.

Ruperta bit her lip angrily, then remembered that as yet no fresh harm had befallen her while in his company. She thought about his voice. It seemed to her that it had changed. It was not the one that he had used earlier when he had held up the coach and robbed her and her companions. Although he had been short in his manner and answers since leaving the scene, she guessed that the voice with which he had spoken to her was his normal one. The former gruff harshness was gone. No doubt part of his disguise.

After another quarter of a mile of riding in silence she could no longer control her curiosity and still smouldering anger. This man owed her an explanation of what was going to happen to her next. But she must choose her words.

'What made you take to this trade of robbing travellers and frightening them? Is there no honest work that you could do?'

His laugh, tinged with bitterness, rang out

amongst the trees. 'This honest work that you mention so easily does not pay so well or so speedily as what you term robbery. And I and others are only getting back that which was ours in the first place.'

'But I and those others have not robbed you,' she protested strongly. 'How can you say that? I've never had dealings with you before, and I shall never again, I hope.'

'You do not understand.'

'I understand well enough,' she retorted hotly. 'And so would you if you had been robbed. You are a thief – a common roadside thief! What am I going to do now? I live in London. How am I going to return there when my money lies jangling in your pocket? Just wait until my father hears of this!'

'And what will he do? Bring an army to rescue you?'

'When he returns from his service with the Fleet, he shall hear of this, I promise. He is a man of power and influence, and will treat the likes of you shortly.'

'And who is this great man you speak of?'

'Prince Rupert.' The name flashed from her lips before she could stop it.

'Prince Rupert?' said her companion in mocking disbelief. He laughed, and she saw the gleam of his teeth. 'I'll say this for you, you've a quick, inventive mind. But you are not very good at lying convincingly.'

Ruperta breathed a sigh of relief. She had not meant to say anything about her father. She must be careful in future. If he had believed her, he might have held her to ransom.

The highwayman addressed her across the darkness between them. 'One thing you forget. Prince Rupert has no daughter, leastways she has never been heard of in these parts. Or, I'll wager, anywhere else. And from what I've heard of him, he'd not be the man to send his daughter on a coach journey with no suitable companion.' He paused before going on: 'There is one thing, though, if and when you get back to London, providing that is where you come from, you can give a message to King Charles. I–'

'Any message you can give him yourself,' Ruperta interrupted.

Her companion carried on evenly as if she had not spoken. 'I would have him know that Royalists everywhere resent the passing of the Act of Indemnity and Oblivion. It has meant indemnity for his enemies and oblivion for the friends who gave all that they had in support of his father and himself. If King Charles cannot or will not repay us, we must take what we can find.'

Ruperta was too full of her own troubles to have much sympathy for the man riding alongside her. An hour ago she had been looking forward to supper and a warm bed in Chodbury. Now, in deep anxiety and with some fear, she was being forced to accompany this highway robber. Her possessions were the clothes she wore and the one coin she had kept back. She had left London hoping to find the house called Ravall's Court, and her mother. But all she could do now was to return home – if, indeed, that was possible. Nevertheless, she was curious to know how near she was to that house, though it now seemed as if she would never see it or her mother.

'You must know this district well,' she said. 'Does the name Ravall's Court mean anything to you?'

'Ravall's Court?' He sounded surprised.

'Yes, the purpose of my journey which you so rudely and violently interrupted was to visit it,' she stated sharply and resentfully.

He did not reply, and Ruperta began to think that either he did not know the place or for some reason he did not wish to tell her about it.

A few minutes later they halted. To

Ruperta's great surprise, her companion said: 'I shall leave you now. You have nothing to fear. Look straight ahead beyond those trees.'

She strained her eyes, and discerned a faint light behind some trees in the distance. It was impossible to tell how far away it was.

'There is a house there. Tell them your tale. They will give you a bed for the night. You will understand that I cannot venture too near dwellings, since I am what I am,' he added dryly.

She heard the jingle of coins.

'Here. I shall be generous this night.' He reached across. 'I cannot return it all to you.'

She pushed his hand away. 'Nothing less than a return of everything you have stolen from me will convince me of your generosity,' she said coldly, and regretted the words the moment they were out of her mouth.

'Don't be too haughty! Take what I offer – the world will be hostile towards you in the morning if you cannot buy your way home again.' He held his hand out again.

This time she allowed him to drop the money into her palm. The metal offered a certain comfort. He was right, she would not get far without some money.

'I'm sorry you hurt your head,' he told her. 'If the fools had not tried to escape me...'

Ruperta refrained from pointing out the weakness of his argument. She could not work up anger again. The sooner she found shelter the better.

'I cannot think of you with anything but ill feeling for what you have done to me,' she said, 'but I hope that you will change your ways before it is too late.'

He chuckled. 'I can assure you that this occupation was not altogether of my choosing, but born of necessity. And now I must leave you.'

He dismounted, saw to makeshift reins for her horse.

'Good-bye,' Ruperta said. She glanced at him, but could see nothing of his face.

'Good-bye, lady. Do not be too harsh in your account of me to others.' He went on with a sudden light-heartedness which surprised her: 'You will agree this sport of mine has its advantages. I am a fisherman on land. I spread my net, and lo, I catch a mermaid. A very pretty one, too.'

She began to move off. The compliment would have pleased her in normal circumstances, but she was too apprehensive just then to care about it.

'I shall remain here a few minutes,' he called out to her. 'Make straight for the light, and you will come to no harm.'

That was considerate of him, she thought. But how strange that she should be gaining comfort from the fact that a highwayman, and furthermore one who had robbed her, was watching her disappear into the darkness! Never in her most unbridled imaginings could she have foreseen the events of the last hour.

She went on carefully, keeping her eyes on the light ahead. Once she glanced back, but could see nothing of the highwayman. She now rode astride, making it less likely that she would fall off. If that happened, it would be difficult to remount, and she was not sure just how far away the house with the light was. She was thankful that she still had the horse, feeling much safer than she would have done making for the house on foot.

The distance turned out to be shorter than it had at first appeared, and soon she was able to see more clearly the trees between which the yellow flickering light showed. As she got nearer, Ruperta saw that it was coming from a downstairs window in the building.

A wide, arched entrance showed dimly to the right of the trees, and Ruperta approached it slowly and apprehensively, not sure what kind of reception she would be given by the occupants of the house.

She became conscious of another sound – a constant murmuring above the movement of the trees, and with it cooler air. She was near the sea.

Beyond the entrance a carriageway led to the house. She halted the animal and sat still before venturing farther. The upper part of the house and its chimneys showed deep black against the night sky. She shivered. It did not look very welcoming.

What was she going to say? Would the occupants of the house believe her, or would they turn her away? Would she be in danger from those who lived there? Yet she needed help, she told herself, shelter for the night until she could make some sort of plan to return to London and home. She had no choice but to place herself at the mercy of the occupants of the house. Then she reflected that the highwayman would not have told her to make for this house if it had been dangerous for her to do so. Perhaps he knew the occupants. Although he was a thief, she did not think that he would have deliberately sent her into unscrupulous and unkindly hands.

As she dismounted, she glimpsed a quickly moving light in the windows above her. She left the horse in an empty outbuilding, and approached the house nervously. The door was set in a porch, and Ruperta, taking a deep breath, knocked timidly upon its solid wood, half hoping now that she would not be heard and that she would be able to steal away.

Moving candlelight appeared in the downstairs windows to her right, then stopped. A few seconds and the light moved lower and became still. Ruperta stepped back a pace at the sound of the bolts being drawn back on the other side of the door. It was a quiet easing of the metal, not a noisy wrenching.

The door opened a little. A female voice said: 'What ails you, John, coming to the front door like this? And why are you back so soon? Are there no travellers abroad this night? One of these–' The voice stopped abruptly as its owner realised that it was not John, whoever he might be, standing there.

Ruperta was so surprised and startled that the door had almost closed again before she could speak. Recovering, she said hastily: 'I am a woman alone and in distress. I mean no harm. I need your help.'

'Who are you?'

'I am called Ruperta.'

'I know no one of that name. And what's a woman doing out alone in these parts in the dark?'

'I was travelling to Chodbury. We were stopped – the coach broke down.'

'Yet you have a horse,' came the quick retort from behind the door.

'I was lent one of the coach horses. I hurt my head, and I am cold and hungry. If you would just allow me to rest awhile...' Ruperta said desperately.

'You spoke of being stopped. How?'

'By a highwayman, who took my money – my ring.'

'A highwayman?' The voice sounded very anxious.

'Yes. I tell you the truth,' said Ruperta in wearied exasperation.

'And he sent you here?' the voice demanded incredulously.

'He pointed me towards the light which showed from here. He thought I would get help. Please allow me to stay the night. I dare not travel alone any farther.'

'You had better go. I cannot let you in.'

The woman was angry and frightened.

In dismay and bewilderment Ruperta stood there. Why was she being refused help? She shivered and pulled her cloak around her tightly. What should she do now? Spend the night in the open and then ride to Chodbury in the morning?

She saw the door closing. 'Then I beg some food from you to take with me,' she said hastily.

Just at that moment a man's voice called from inside the house: 'Who's there? Is that you, Jane?'

'Yes, Father.'

'What is the matter?'

The light which the man carried revealed the fair hair of his daughter as she stood by the door.

Ruperta, seeing no likelihood of success with the daughter, seized her chance, bending forward and addressing the man. Her words tumbled out rapidly and with great anxiety. 'Sir, I beg you to give me shelter for the night, or at least let me warm myself. A highwayman held up the coach – your daughter does not believe me.'

'She's a gipsy, Father, like as not. She has a horse with her.'

Ruperta turned on the speaker in a rush of

anger. 'How dare you! I am not a gipsy. I was a passenger in the coach to Chodbury from Kinnerton. It broke down when the driver attempted to outrun a highwayman.'

'I am sorry my daughter spoke hastily,' said the man gently. 'But the night is plagued with rascals of all kinds, as you have obviously found out.' He frowned. 'But the horse that my daughter says you have. How…?' He broke off.

Relief spread in Ruperta. He had not turned her away. 'Though the highwayman robbed my companions and myself, he showed consideration for my being a woman. It is a coach horse that he ordered the others to set me on.' She was aware of the hostile stare of the young woman upon her.

Evidently Ruperta's account and her distressed appearance impressed the man. The candle moved towards her and back again. 'Come in, then. I think we can find you room for this night. And someone will see to the horse.'

'Oh, I shall remember your kindness, sir,' she sighed in utter thankfulness and gratitude as she entered the porch.

He turned and led the way into the house. Ruperta was conscious of his daughter's eyes boring into her back. She did not care.

She was inside – out of the lonely and dangerous darkness.

Red embers were glowing in the fire-place of the large room into which she was taken. The man bade her sit in a chair by the hearth, then picked up three logs and threw them on the fire. Then he turned to his daughter. 'Jane! Go tell your mother we have a visitor.'

The girl, with a tightening of the lips, did as she was told, but reluctantly, climbing the staircase slowly to disappear into the darkness above.

The man looked at Ruperta with some concern. 'The fire will soon burn up. Warm yourself. No doubt the shock and the night will have made you cold. I shall go into the kitchen. We must have something left from supper.' He went on apologetically: 'We have not much to offer a guest these days, but what we have you are welcome to share.'

Ruperta was apologetic in turn. 'I would not have troubled you, sir, had I not been afraid of what might happen to me. The highwayman pointed out your house, and told me to seek help.'

'Most considerate of him after robbing you.' He smiled with sympathetic wryness, then left her for a few moments. Ruperta basked in the growing flame and heat of the fire, then glanced towards the stairs. An indistinct face stared over the rail at her. Startled for the moment, she continued to gaze, and the face vanished.

The man appeared again with a pan which he rested on a grid across the fire, then he placed the light upon the table in the centre of the room. 'Lamb stew – it will not take long to heat,' he said.

Her host was tall, fair and angular. He must have been very handsome when young, she thought. Still was, but furrows on the brow and strain lines in the thin cheeks hinted at a troubled mind.

CHAPTER TWO

The stairs creaked and Ruperta saw Jane descending, with another woman, presumably her mother, behind her. When they reached the bottom, the girl went to stand by the fire, her eyes moving about Ruperta unceasingly and suspiciously.

The older woman came from the shadows of the stairs into the room. She was just under medium height, plump, and carried herself proudly. She was dark of hair and complexion. When she drew near, the firelight was caught and held in the large brown eyes which were fixed on Ruperta.

A comforting, sympathetic face, contrasting with that of her daughter, the visitor reflected.

The man said, smiling at his wife: 'Ann, meet our visitor from the night. The coach was held up and she was robbed.' He glanced from one to the other. 'This is my wife, Ann Colston. I am Jeremy Colston.' He nodded towards the fire-place. 'Our daughter, Jane.'

'And I am—' Ruperta hesitated. She disliked the name Ruperta; had always wanted to be called Elizabeth. Now she had the chance. 'Elizabeth – Elizabeth Wittel,' she said firmly. Her father was of the House of Wittelsbach, but in England she thought it better not to use the name in full.

Ann Colston extended her hand in welcome. 'You must stay until you are recovered from the ordeal, Mistress Wittel. Are you unharmed?'

'I hit my head when the carriage was damaged; but the soreness is wearing off. Thank you for taking me in. I do not know what I should have done otherwise, though I regret that I have kept you from your bed.'

Mrs Colston smiled Ruperta's apology away. 'My husband had just bolted the doors.' She glanced at Jane. 'My daughter, I am afraid, keeps later hours. Sometimes it is gone twelve before she is abed. Though I must confess to doing my share of watching from the gallery windows for my husband when I was young.' She touched his arm and smiled tenderly at him.

Fleeting annoyance crossed her daughter's face. 'You know, Mother, that I sleep badly at times, and then I watch for John's return.'

Mrs Colston nodded, and Ruperta observed that the mention of John's name had caused her hostess to look anxious. She turned to Ruperta. 'John is our son,' she explained. 'I wish he would not stay out so late. It is too far to go to Chodbury to meet friends, and he has taken instead to riding along the shore at night, since it eases his mind before sleep.'

The contents of the pan upon the fire began to bubble, and her husband moved quickly towards it. 'I had for the moment forgotten about the stew,' he said. 'Our guest will think us lacking in hospitality.'

'Just to sit by your fire is welcome to me,' Ruperta said gratefully. She was feeling more comfortable, and her headache had almost gone.

Mrs Colston took the pan from her husband, ladled the contents into a bowl while he disappeared into the shadows at the other end of the great room. He was soon back with a silver goblet which he set down alongside the bowl, saying: 'Now Mistress Wittel, you can eat and drink.' Then he added with sad bitterness: 'Once we had silver and servants. Now we have little silver and no servants.'

Ruperta guessed what had happened to the family fortunes. So many Royalist households were in the same state of poverty. In the flickering candlelight and with the fire warm upon her back she ate and drank; once she glanced up to find Mrs Colston observing her with a wondering look...

When she had finished, Ruperta told them more fully what had happened to her from the time of the highwayman's appearance, and added that she was on her way to Chodbury from London.

'Then you're a long way from home, Mistress Wittel,' observed Mr Colston with some concern.

'And have you relations in this part of the country that you came so far?' inquired Mrs Colston politely.

Ruperta could hardly explain that she had come in search of her mother. If word ever reached her father's ears of what she was doing, his temper would know no bounds. 'No,' she answered. 'I was hoping to reach Plymouth.' She went on, surprised at her own glibness: 'My father was a soldier – he died on the Continent. He came from Plymouth, and told me many times that I should visit it. The little money he left me and some I had saved during my work in London was to enable me to do as my father wished.'

'You poor, unfortunate girl,' murmured Mrs Colston in great sympathy.

'And I am sorry, Mistress Wittel,' said Mr Colston, 'that your misfortunes should occur in this part of the realm. It is to be hoped that the thief is caught and given what he deserves, and that you get your money back, though I doubt it – it will be spent by now, for a thief's quick gains are just as quickly spent.'

'You are very brave to journey so far alone,' said Mrs Colston in admiration. 'There are discomforts and dangers for travellers on the highway today.'

Jane, who had been carefully studying the visitor, said abruptly: 'I thought you were in league with some highwayman. That was the reason for my not wanting you here, that and the horse.' There was a slight softening in her manner and tone of voice.

For her part, Ruperta felt there had been some other reason, but it was, after all, no concern of hers now. She was also aware of the many uneasy glances the daughter had thrown towards the window. Was it her brother she was looking and listening for?

Ruperta told herself that it must have been upsetting and alarming to have a stranger demanding entrance on a dark night. 'I apologise, Mistress Colston, if I was uncivil towards you earlier. I was upset and distressed by what had happened.'

Jane pushed her long, fair hair back from her forehead with both hands. A slight smile acknowledged the apology and softened her features. She was a tall girl and bore a striking likeness to her father.

Her question, voiced in puzzled tones which contained an element of distrust, caught Ruperta unprepared. 'You say that your first name is Elizabeth?'

Ruperta nodded, smiling.

'Why, then, did you call yourself by another name when you demanded entrance of me?'

Ruperta felt the eyes of the others upon her. 'Because that is the name that I was given at birth. My real name. But I do not like it, I prefer to be called Elizabeth,' she explained.

'What is this name that you do not like?' asked Mr Colston with interest.

'Ruperta,' she replied, giving him a small, wry smile. She heard a gasp, and swung round. To her utter surprise Mrs Colston was leaning forward rigidly, hands locked together.

'Ruperta.' The sound was a whispered mixture of shock, fear and incredulity. Her eyes clung deeply questioning to her visitor's.

40

Then Mrs Colston's gaze lost its intentness, and she slumped in her chair, her body as limp as it had been rigid seconds before.

Ruperta jumped from her seat just in time to stop Mrs Colston from sliding on to the floor. And with Mr Colston's help she managed to get his wife upright in her chair again.

Jane Colston rushed to her mother's side, throwing an accusing glance at Ruperta.

The older woman's eyes fluttered open, but she remained still and silent, not looking at any of them.

'What ails you, Ann? Tell me, please,' pleaded Mr Colston, bending down, trying to look into her face.

Still without looking at anyone, she said: 'It must have been my thoughts of the danger to John at this hour. The knocking on the door frightened me.'

'Oh, I am sorry, Mrs Colston,' said Ruperta hastily.

'Do not blame yourself,' said her hostess. 'I have been tired lately, worried. I have not…'

'Nevertheless, Ann,' broke in Mr Colston in sudden anger, 'I shall be bound to forbid my son's nightly wandering from now on. I will not have you upset and made ill.'

41

She put out a hand wearily, placatingly. 'No, Jeremy, no. He is a man now. We must accept that.'

Again Ruperta sensed that not all the truth was being told…

'I think I shall go to bed now,' said Mrs Colston unsteadily. 'You will forgive me, Mistress Wittel. It is not like me to faint away…'

'I blame myself for it, Mrs Colston. I feel that I am responsible,' Ruperta said.

For the first time since she had fainted the older woman looked straight into Ruperta's face. Her dark eyes held a searching intentness. 'I shall be well enough in the morning,' she murmured with a strained smile. She turned to her daughter. 'See that our guest is made comfortable, Jane.'

Good nights were exchanged, and then Mr Colston put his arm round his wife's shoulders, and together they climbed the stairs out of sight. Ruperta heard a door closing.

Jane moved towards the stairs and Ruperta hesitated, not sure whether to follow immediately. Then Jane halted and looked over her shoulder at Ruperta. 'Your bed lies this way, Mistress Two Names,' she said sourly.

Ruperta bit back a sharp reply. She would, after all, be leaving in the morning. She found it strange that kind, gentle and hospitable people like the Colstons should have such a boorish, graceless daughter. Why was she so much on edge? What did she expect to see outside the windows she had glanced through so often when she was not studying Ruperta herself? And now it seemed that Jane wanted her out of the way as quickly as possible.

Jane led the way upstairs, and along a passage to a door facing them at the far end. Then she pushed the door open and stood aside, holding up the candle. The flickering light showed a small room, the greater part of it in shadow, but two narrow windows gave some light from the night sky outside.

'The bed is over there,' Jane said curtly. Ruperta could just make out its shape against the far wall. The light behind her moved away. She turned quickly as the door began to close upon her.

'Oh, Mistress Colston!' she called softly.

'Yes?' The voice was impatient.

'I am curious to know where I am. What is the name of this house?'

There was a moment's silence. 'For a stranger passing by, you are out of the ordinary inquisitive, Mistress Wittel.' The words were quick, jerky, the tone resentful.

'And you, Mistress Colston, as the daughter of the house, whatever its name, are out of the ordinary ill-mannered,' retorted Ruperta in sudden indignation. 'All I wanted was to know where I received kindness. Some day I might be able to repay it.' She turned away, already regretting her momentary loss of temper.

The door opened a fraction wider. 'Ravall's Court.' The words were flung at her grudgingly. 'Now you can sleep satisfied.'

Ruperta was not aware of the door banging shut or of Jane's footsteps hurrying away. She leaned against the windows looking out unseeingly, the stone of the mullion striking cold on her palms. How long she stood there she had no idea. Thoughts crowded into her mind so that it was impossible for her to distinguish one from another.

Ann Colston had fainted on hearing Ruperta's name. And even before that, there had been that strange, puzzled expression on the older woman's face. She must have guessed, and the shock had been too much for her. She, Ruperta, had spoken with her mother after all those years.

So Jane must be her half-sister; the John they had mentioned would be her half-brother. Dizzy with thinking, she lay on the bed fully dressed and huddled under her cloak. Sleep would be a long time coming if ever it did come.

Ruperta remembered the angry and frightened face of Jane at the door. Why had she been so unkind to a person seeking help and shelter? It was true that any person, even a woman coming to the door after dark had to be regarded with suspicion, but Jane's manner had been that of a woman already in a state of fear. And her more than anxious waiting for her brother – had it really been for him or for someone else? And why had she been so reluctant to give the name of the house to a guest who was staying for one night only? What possible harm could there be in that?

Ruperta drifted off into a fitful sleep. For how long she did not know, but she was awakened by the sound of voices coming from outside her window. She rose, shivering in the night air, and went to the window, but she was unable to see anyone. The voices below were those of a man and woman, hers in alarmed and angry rebuke, his in lower placatory tones. Ruperta caught a few words '…see to the coach horse…'

The voices faded away, the sound of hoof beats with them, to the left of where

45

Ruperta's forehead pressed against the cold glass. She thought of the horse she had arrived on, and was ashamed that she had forgotten about the poor beast. It seemed, however, that it was now being cared for.

Ruperta sighed wearily and returned to bed, still with her clothes on. The last picture in her mind before she eventually fell asleep was that of her mother...

Discreet knocking awakened Ruperta the next morning. It took her several moments to recollect where she was.

'It's Mrs Colston, Mistress Wittel,' came from the other side of the door. 'I have brought hot water for you.'

'Th-thank you,' called Ruperta. 'Have I slept late?'

'It is about ten, but that is a matter of no concern. The weather would not tempt any-one to rise early.'

Ruperta was aware of heavy rain beating against the windows. She arose quickly, throwing her cloak round her shoulders. 'Please come in, Mrs Colston,' she called, taking a step towards the door. She could not keep a note of excitement from creeping into her voice. This was her mother, she was sure, coming like a servant with water for her!

She watched as the door opened, saw the

figure stoop to lift the jug and bowl from the floor, and went to help as Mrs Colston entered the room. For seconds Ruperta was aware only of the large brown eyes gazing straight into hers. Then taking the jug and bowl, she placed them on a chest near the window.

The door closed behind her, and when she turned round again Mrs Colston was just inside the room, staring at her rather shyly.

'Are – are you feeling better this morning, Mrs Colston?' the girl said.

The older woman smiled, her teeth showing white against her dark complexion. 'Much better, I thank you. But what you must think of me!'

'A great deal, I can assure you, but none of it badly,' said Ruperta steadily. She saw the other's glance at her attire. 'I was so tired that I just fell into bed without undressing.' She pushed at her hair. 'You must think me a sad sight, Mrs Colston.'

The other shook her head firmly, regarding Ruperta closely the while. She appeared to be having difficulty in making up her mind about something, a frown coming and going and her hands clasping and unclasping agitatedly. Finally she glanced at the closed door then back at Ruperta.

'I scarcely dare to ask for fear of getting the wrong answer, Mistress Wittel,' she said in little above a whisper. 'But if my questions offend you, or you do not understand, I beseech you to forget my words.'

The girl just nodded, all else forgotten except herself and her companion.

Intensely serious, her eyes fixed rigidly on Ruperta's, Mrs Colston said huskily: 'Just – just tell me one thing. Is your – your father Prince Rupert, nephew to the late King Charles?'

'Yes.'

'You have not known your mother?'

'No, but I do now,' the girl whispered.

Her mother's face was transformed. Joy, bewilderment, anxiety, and pride showed on it. Her hands grasped Ruperta's, and she shook her head at her failure to find words.

Ruperta pulled her mother suddenly to her, her tears dampening her newly found parent's hair.

Just for seconds they embraced each other, then her mother drew away quickly, glancing back at the door. 'I must go. They must never know.' She dabbed at her eyes, then looked at Ruperta. 'I realised last night. The shock was too much for me. I did not sleep for thinking of you.' She swallowed, took a deep breath and moved towards the door. 'Come down to breakfast in the kitchen. When the others are gone, we shall talk together ... Ruperta.'

With another dab at her eyes and another quick glance at her daughter she was gone, leaving Ruperta staring after her.

The speed with which she had found her mother had confused her emotionally. Events had, in a matter of hours, thrown her into the heart of the very family she had set out to find...

Later, having washed, and then tidied herself as best she could, she went downstairs. She would have felt happier had she had a change of clothing, but her baggage had been lashed to the top of the coach. If it had been left unattended her belongings would probably have been stolen by now.

Ruperta reached the bottom of the stairs and stood for a moment in the great hall, the room into which she had been led the night before. Most of it had been impossible to see in the candlelight then; in the daytime it appeared much larger. A fire blazed on the hearth, a cheering sight in contrast to the miserable weather outside.

She crossed the hall to the windows at the other side, knelt on the wooden seat and rubbed a portion of window clear of mist. Beneath she saw a path, and beyond it a garden sloping gently downwards. Trees stood sentinel to left and right, their top-most branches waving in wet helplessness. In the distance she could make out the sea with its white crests.

'Should you not be informing your mistress that a visitor has arrived?' said a voice from behind her.

She gasped, and swung round. Just inside the doorway from the porch stood a man, quite still, watching her. He was tall, and wore a wide-brimmed hat, his black cloak was open showing his maroon doublet and breeches and bucket-topped black boots.

Ruperta was irritated by his tone. 'No, I should not. I am a guest, not a servant,' she replied sharply. 'I shall however, inform someone of your arrival.' She began to turn away.

He shook his head. 'It does not matter. I can see now that on no account could you be mistaken for a servant.'

Ruperta remained where she was, frowning. She looked down at herself and sighed. 'Small wonder that you took me for a servant! These clothes are the only ones that I possess. I travelled in them yesterday. I was

50

waylaid by a highwayman on the road to Chodbury yesterday. By now my baggage has probably been stolen as well.'

'I'm sorry to hear of your misfortune. Some people make their living in a strange way,' the visitor said.

He came forward, taking off his hat in a wide, sweeping flourish to reveal golden hair which was burnished by the firelight. 'I am Roger Sudworth. I see I startled you and, what is more, annoyed you – your pardon for that.' He glanced past her to the window behind. 'Something was engaging your attention out there, though I cannot think what it can have been on such a morning.' Eyes of a summer sky blue rested their twinkling gaze on her.

Recovering herself and feeling slightly foolish, Ruperta smiled at him. 'I am Ruperta Wittel.' She held out her hand; he took it, and bowed over it. 'I – I was trying to glimpse the sea,' she said.

Roger Sudworth unfastened his cloak, flung the wet garment over the banisters, then shied his hat at the top of the lower stair post where it clung momentarily, then fell to the floor. He bent to retrieve it, placed it firmly on the post, and glanced back at Ruperta.

'I fear that I need more practice,' he said with a grin.

He made for the fire and stood to one side of it. He indicated the chair opposite, smiled apologetically. 'Please, Mistress Wittel, be seated. My manners are getting as bad as my aim. Or am I detaining you from something?'

Ruperta shook her head, sat down. It was pleasant by the fire. 'I think the others believe that I am still abed.' She must tell them that they had a visitor, but there was no hurry, she decided.

He turned slightly away from her, warming his hands, and she studied him. His suit was of a rich velvet, his cravat and cuffs were trimmed with fine lace. His appearance and manners spoke of wealth and a carefree existence. She wondered why he had come, and what his connection with the Colston family was.

'So you met a gentleman of the road, did you?' he said suddenly.

'A heartless rogue is a better description.' She frowned at the memory, then her face cleared. 'Though he did me a kindness – I know not why.'

'Oh, what was that?' said her companion with polite interest.

'He put me on one of the coach horses, guided me here and gave me a handful of my own money back.'

'A very considerate gentleman it would seem,' Roger Sudworth remarked.

'He was a common thief who ruined my journey and frightened me! My clothes are lost. Most of my money is gone, along with something I valued above all else.'

'Oh?' Roger Sudworth said sharply.

'The thief took the ring that my father gave me. I treasured it because although I do not see him often it was a link between us, and...' She broke off, almost in tears.

Roger Sudworth looked away, and she was glad. 'It appears,' he said thoughtfully, 'that your highwayman friend in his haste to gather riches overlooked such niceties. I'm sure when he thinks about it, he will regret it.'

Ruperta smiled ruefully. 'It will have been exchanged for money and drink, no doubt.' She shrugged. 'That is the end of it. I shall have to forget the affair.'

There was a silence between them. Ruperta broke it, frowning. 'But why, why did he do it?'

'He probably needed money,' the young man said. 'To keep out of a debtors' prison is as good a reason as any.'

'He did not sound poor,' Ruperta said slowly.

'Can you tell poverty by the sound, Mistress Wittel?' He regarded her quizzically, and added: 'He may have regarded it as a kind of dare.'

She looked at him in surprise. 'I do not understand.'

'A man needs a challenge – a tilt at authority – otherwise he rusts away.'

Ruperta thought of her father. He was one who delighted in a challenge. But she was not going to give her companion the satisfaction of hearing her admit that he could be right. 'Then all I can say,' she said curtly, 'is that a man should have more important things to do.'

Roger Sudworth spread his arms wide, then let them flop to his sides with a look of reproach. 'For myself, I am not without money, and I am occupied too fully to have time for challenges. In addition I have not the nerve for such a dangerous game.'

With that he went across and picked up his cloak and hat, then turned back to Ruperta. 'It is probable that a search is being made for you. I am going as far as Chodbury now. Shall I make it known that you have reached safety and have not been kidnapped by that ruffian?'

Ruperta thought quickly. The quieter her visit to that particular house was kept the better. 'I should be obliged, Mr Sudworth, if you would simply let it be known that I am safe. Say nothing of my whereabouts unless you are forced.'

He nodded, then flung his cloak around his shoulders. 'Do you intend to stay here a while?' he asked.

Ruperta was mildly surprised at his question. 'It does not rest with me, Mr Sudworth, though I would be glad to spend another night here, I admit.'

Roger Sudworth smiled cheerfully. 'Then perhaps we shall meet again, Mistress Wittel.' He turned towards the porch door.

Ruperta rose from her chair, took a step after him. 'But did you not wish to speak with Mrs Colston or someone? Shall I say that you are here.'

He shook his head. 'I was just passing by.' The blue eyes danced merrily. Before she had realised what he meant to do, he had bent forward and kissed her gently on the lips.

By the time she had recovered herself he was opening the door of the porch. 'It is a short life, Mistress Wittel. We must take advantage of the opportunities given us. If my horse should trample on me within the hour, I should take the memory of that kiss with me.' The door closed behind him.

She remained where she was, her face flushed with anger. As he approached his horse, another rider came into view and Ruperta stepped to the window to see better.

The newcomer dismounted, and the two men stood a yard or so apart. Even at a distance, Ruperta sensed the strained atmosphere between them. The conversation did not last long, then the second man came towards the house. As she watched, Roger Sudworth mounted his horse, and with a flourish of his hat in her direction galloped off, seemingly undismayed by the other's reception of him.

Ruperta found that she had her hands to her mouth. To keep the feeling of his lips upon hers from fading away? She dismissed the thought from her mind, but she felt uneasy...

As she moved away from the window she wondered who this second man was. Could it be John Colston – her half-brother?'

He came into the hall, but did not appear to see her immediately. He was scowling and moving his lips as if quite out of temper.

She stepped forward, smiling pleasantly. 'Are you Mr John Colston?'

He nodded, and took off his old-fashioned, tall-crowned hat and his long, voluminous black cloak from which water dripped to the floor. The ruddy face under the hat glistened from the moisture upon it. He brought with him the smell of rain.

She held out her hand. 'I am Mistress Wittel. I was given shelter in the house last night, after having been waylaid and robbed. Your parents have been very kind.'

'I am sorry for your loss,' he said, giving her a somewhat strange look. Then he moved nearer the hearth, and hung his hat and cloak on a peg by the side of the fire-place. Ruperta saw that his clothes had once been good, but were now long past their best.

'When are you thinking of leaving, Mistress Wittel?' He glanced at her, then looked away to the window.

Ruperta was surprised at his question. His manner was polite, but she caught a note of anxiety. 'Tomorrow,' she replied.

His eyes jerked back to her momentarily. 'I mean – if your parents consent,' she went on quickly. 'I shall feel more recovered after another night here.'

He nodded, looking at the floor.

'If it is inconvenient, I shall…' she began.

He gave a swift shake of his head. 'I would have escorted you into Chodbury, had you been leaving today – that is why I asked.'

Somehow Ruperta did not think that had been the real reason for his question. His auburn hair framed an open, pleasant face. Yet he had avoided looking at her directly for most of their short conversation.

He nodded towards the window. 'D'you know the man who has just gone?' he asked, a trifle suspiciously.

'I have never met him before in my life. He came in unannounced. I was about to enter the kitchen. Do you know him?'

John Colston's gaze remained steady on her. 'Aye, I know him. Never did I think to see him here again,' he muttered grimly. 'What did he want?'

Ruperta showed her puzzlement. 'I don't know. He told me he was Roger Sudworth. I gave him my name, told him why I was here.' She gave a shrug. 'We spoke of high-waymen, in particular of the rogue who had caused me such distress.'

He half turned away from her, frowning heavily, his eyes moving restlessly about him. Then, evidently having made up his mind

58

about something, he said briskly: 'We shall meet again later perhaps, Mistress Wittel,' and with that he strode off in the direction of the kitchen. Ruperta saw its door close behind him and heard the subdued sound of voices beyond.

She stood by the fire, her mind busy. So that was John, her half-brother. How glad she would have been if she could have introduced herself openly! But she could not...

She was beginning to feel hungry, and would have liked to have gone into the kitchen with John, but she did not want to intrude on what seemed to be a family talk. Her mother would probably come and look for her when the conversation ended.

Some five minutes passed, then John Colston appeared again and beckoned her into the kitchen. 'My mother is sorry that you should stand out there, you should have come in,' he told Ruperta, then made off across the hall without another word.

Ruperta stood in the doorway, a renewed excitement mounting at seeing her mother again.

Ann Colston glanced up, and smiled a welcome. 'Mistress Wittel! Come in, you must be hungry. You did not have much to eat last night.' She seemed to have recovered from the deep emotion she had displayed earlier.

Ann turned to the other occupant of the kitchen, an elderly, white-haired man who sat at the head of the table at the back of the room. 'Father,' she said, her voice very loud and clear, 'this is Mistress Wittel, the lady who was waylaid by the highwayman last night.' She looked at Ruperta. 'This is my father, Sir Peter Ravall. His age and deafness give me concern, but at times he hears more than I think he can.' She regarded him with great affection and some sadness.

'Good morning to you, Sir Peter,' Ruperta said brightly.

She felt as if in a dream. This was her grandfather, now lifting himself stiffly and with difficulty to his feet. He was not in the least like his daughter, but there was humour as well as pride in the strong features, and Ruperta felt that he would be a very present help in time of trouble.

He drew himself up, then bowed and extended his hand.

'Good morning to you, Mistress Wittel, and a better day, I hope, than you had yesterday.' His brown eyes looked straight into hers, then flickered quickly over her features. A slightly puzzled frown appeared on his brow.

'You have a likeness to my own daughter when she was about your age.' His eyes twinkled. 'But it is considered poor taste to ask about a lady's age – whether she is young or old.'

'I am in my twenty-second year, sir,' Ruperta said, smiling at him. She liked Sir Peter, she had decided.

He turned to his daughter. 'Do you not notice this likeness yourself, Ann?'

Ruperta saw the warning in her mother's eyes as they met her own. They would have to be careful. Sir Peter must have known about Prince Rupert and Ann, but there was nothing to be said for reviving old unhappiness.

'A superficial likeness, Father,' said Mrs Colston rather hurriedly, 'but there it ends. She is a very pretty girl.'

She turned away, but not before Ruperta had glimpsed the emotion in her face. 'And if I do not,' she went on, 'provide her with food this very minute she will faint, and that is no good recommendation for this house. Please sit down, Mistress Wittel.' She moved towards the fire, obviously intending to deny Sir Peter the opportunity of comparing the two of them side by side.

However, it did not stop his questioning when he heard that she had come from London. He wanted to know about the plague, and about the victory of the King's ships over the Dutch. Despite constant pain from an old head wound, Prince Rupert had commanded one of the English squadrons, and had led the Fleet into battle. Ruperta knew a great deal, but she would have to be wary of disclosing the extent of her knowledge. She and her mother did not want Sir Peter to suspect that there was any connection between the Prince and Mistress Wittel.

During the conversation with Sir Peter, Ann Colston busied herself with preparing her daughter's meal. It was obvious to the girl that her mother gave the closest possible attention to what was being said.

When she placed the food on the table in front of Ruperta, Sir Peter remarked somewhat bitterly: 'Once no guest would have eaten in the kitchen. Times have changed.'

No doubt, thought Ruperta, the household had suffered under Cromwell's rule. Supporters of Charles I had hoped that his son would make good the losses they had sustained. But Charles II would have required a bottomless purse to settle all the claims made on him. The money simply was not there.

The old man rose from the table. 'You will excuse me, Mistress Wittel, but I never miss my daily walk around the house, whatever the weather. I go no farther now, but I feel that if I break the habit, I shall be bound to my chair and then to my bed for ever.' He smiled rather grimly, and added: 'I am in no mood for that to happen yet.'

Ruperta glanced out of the window. He would get drenched in no time. She wondered where the others were. She had neither seen nor heard of Jane or Mr Colston that morning.

The two women watched Sir Peter as he made his way slowly to the kitchen door.

'Could you not leave it this once?' asked his daughter anxiously. 'It rains heavily, perhaps later it will…'

'No, Ann,' he interrupted firmly, 'you know it is my pleasure.'

'It is little of a pleasure that I can see,' she said, 'but be all the more careful, and wear your cloak to protect you.' She fetched it and carefully fastened it for him.

Sir Peter looked back from the door at Ruperta. 'No doubt we shall be able to talk again, Mistress Wittel. You will not be gone awhile yet.' There was a twinkle in his eyes as he said: 'The weather is far too bad for a

London dweller to venture out.'

Hardly had the door shut behind him than Mrs Colston had hastened to the table where she seated herself opposite Ruperta. 'Now we can talk, Ruperta, without fear of interruption.' She reached across to take hold of her daughter's hand. 'Please do not think ill of me for letting you go as a child, Ruperta. The Prince and my father had you taken away from here soon after you were born. Not long afterwards my marriage to Jeremy Colston was arranged. He is a good, kind person; I soon learned to love him as he deserved. But no woman ever quite forgets the man who first won her heart.'

Ruperta observed the rising colour in her mother's cheeks, her fingers moving restlessly as she talked. 'I cannot excuse what I did, but I can explain ... perhaps. Your father was every inch a king's son – and he had so many inches! He was also a young knight errant riding out to right his uncle's wrongs. Half the women in England were in love with him. You do understand?'

Ruperta nodded in growing affection and reached out to squeeze her mother's arm in a gesture of sympathetic understanding.

'I would not have come seeking you in this manner if I had felt ill disposed towards you.

So often have I thought of you, Mother. I shall call you that when we are alone together.' She smiled tenderly. 'I am so happy to have found you.'

Ann Colston gave a little sigh of relief at these words. 'I used to wonder where you were, what you would be doing. The daughter of Prince Rupert.' She grasped Ruperta's hand in both of hers. 'He was a very handsome man, your father,' she went on softly, half smiling. The reflective look gave way suddenly to a proud one. 'Did you know he asked me to marry him? And before he knew I was bearing his child.'

There was a silence between them for a few moments; they looked at each other with understanding and sympathy...

'So Sir Peter knew about me?' said Ruperta.

'Yes. I tried to keep the knowledge from him but it was impossible. I was foolish to think I could deceive him for long. He was very kind to me; my mother, had she still been alive, could not have been kinder; and he told me that I had been right to refuse the Prince. Think what King Charles would have said if confronted with a niece by marriage neither wealthy nor nobly born!'

'May not your father suspect who I am?'

Ruperta said anxiously.

'It is doubtful,' replied her mother, 'though he did pass that remark about the resemblance between us. On the whole, I hope that he will not find out. He would be glad to have met his grandchild; on the other hand he might, in his excitement, let the secret out to the others.' She looked deep into Ruperta's eyes. 'I love Jeremy, and even after all this time, he may hold it against me if he finds out. He may not forgive me. I cannot tell anyone my secret, though for many reasons I wish that I could.'

CHAPTER THREE

All the time her mother had been talking, Ruperta had been trying to fix every detail of her in her memory, so that later she could picture her in her mind's eye when home in London. No wonder her father had fallen in love with her. She was still very attractive.

Ann Colston was saying: 'When I was your age I was quite like you. But you are very much prettier than I was.'

Ruperta shook her head, smiling deprecatingly, but Ann went on with a sigh: 'You are taller, very graceful. Your father is very tall.'

They continued to gaze at each other, lost in the wonder of their meeting, and hardly believing that it was real.

Ann wanted to know all about her old love, and Ruperta told her at some length.

'Does he know that you have come here?' Ann said suddenly.

'No!' cried Ruperta. 'What he would say if he knew, I cannot bring myself to think.'

'You have come without his knowledge?' her mother whispered incredulously.

67

'He does not see me each day. Sometimes it is weeks between visits. Besides, he is with the King and is likely to remain with him for some time – unless he has to return to the Fleet.'

Her mother sighed. 'Does your father often speak of me?'

'No, I have had to press and harry him to tell me anything at all.'

'Oh.' There was a shade of disappointment in the voice. 'I was a country girl of no importance, to be forgotten, though he did ask me to marry him.'

Ruperta shook her head. 'No, although he does not speak of you, he still remembers. I can tell from the way he has looked sometimes when I have questioned him.'

'Are you certain?' her mother asked doubtfully. Even so there was a new and glad light in her eyes.

Ruperta nodded and said: 'Note that he has never married, though rumour would have had him wedded several times.'

After that Ann wanted to know how Ruperta had found her, and the girl told her about the visit to the midwife.

Ann smiled. 'She will be old now, poor thing. Say discreetly that I have asked after her, and that she is remembered. How

68

thankful I am that she told you of this house! If not, you and I would not have been together like this.' Her mother stood up, leaned far across the table, cupped Ruperta's face in her hands and planted a kiss in the middle of her forehead.

Ruperta, somewhat overcome for the moment, said nothing.

Ann sat back at her own side of the table again. 'If only you could stay,' she sighed hopelessly.

Ruperta said gently: 'It would be best if I went as I came – suddenly – and left you in peace. I am satisfied that I have found you. We can be together in thought. Besides, you have Jane. Had you forgotten that?'

Mrs Colston gave an almost imperceptible shake of her head. 'I love her, too, though of late she has seemed very cross and very unhappy.'

Ruperta had seen as much for herself, but she said nothing.

Ann said more cheerfully: 'Come along now, Ruperta, enough of me. I want to know everything that has happened to you since you left here.'

Ruperta smiled. 'It would take a long time in the telling. But I'll do my best.'

Ann listened intently to all her daughter

had to say, asking an occasional question.

Ruperta in turn learned that Sir Peter had distinguished himself at Bristol, and then heard all about the Colston family and Ann's marriage to Jeremy.

When they had finished exchanging information and memories, Ann looked out at the pouring rain and said: 'It is not fit for you to travel. This bad weather shows no signs of easing.'

They regarded each other, Ruperta knowing from the sudden brightening of her mother's face what she was going to say.

'Why not delay until tomorrow, Ruperta? The day may be fairer. Besides, a few hours is not enough to get to know my daughter.'

Ruperta would have liked nothing better. 'But the others,' she said anxiously, 'they may suspect. A stranger staying on?'

'No, the weather is your excuse.' Her mother's face was eager now. 'They will not suspect. And have you forgotten – your head was hurt and you had suffered shock?'

Ruperta smiled. 'You have persuaded me very easily. Nothing would please me more.' Even so, a little doubt still remained in her. Somehow she did not think that Jane Colston would welcome her remaining there another day.

Then it occurred to Ruperta that her mother had not mentioned the visit of Roger Sudworth. She asked about the young man.

Ann Colston did not answer at once. When she did, it was with a worried and reflective look, and very quietly as if to herself. 'They used to be such friends as young boys. Now I fear that John bears hate towards Roger. And without cause.'

There were footsteps outside in the hall. 'That will be Father back from his walk,' said Ann. 'He will go into the parlour now. It is his habit. You stay here, Ruperta, but I must prepare for the return of Jeremy and Jane.'

'Let me come and help you,' Ruperta said at once.

'No, you are a guest here. But I am glad to see that you are a dutiful and helpful girl.'

An idea struck Ruperta. 'I shall look round the house where I was born.'

Her mother smiled. 'And then you may take away in your memory the house and those of us in it.'

Ruperta kissed her mother and went into the hall. She became aware that the rain had ceased its beating upon the windows, and decided that a walk outside would do her good. A few minutes later, after collecting

71

her cloak, she left by the porch door. It was not as cold as she had thought it would be, and the gentle drizzle caressed her face.

She sighed as she observed everywhere the signs of poverty and neglect. Nothing had been spent on the house for a very long time, and a rose garden opposite the gable-end bore signs of previous care and order, but now flourished wild and unattended.

As she made her way round to the other side, she thought that Ravall's Court was indeed a troubled house.

She could hear the sea quite plainly now, feel the breeze as she left the path and went down to the shingle. She stopped before going nearer the water, seeing the low, rocky sides of the inlet. The tide was going out.

She crossed the sand and walked along the edge of the water slowly, then back again, thinking of nothing in particular, and enjoying the solitude. After a little, she came upon another path leading back to the house, and started to walk along it.

It was then that she noticed what looked like a cave entrance in the base of the rock wall on her right hand.

Feeling curious, she stepped inside. The cave was about a dozen feet in length but roughly half that in width, narrowing some-

72

what towards its rear. A small rock with a flat top stood in the middle of the cave. Light filtered into the gloom from outside, only the innermost few feet being in near darkness.

The glint of something on the wall near the back of the cave caught her eye. Cautiously she moved inwards. To her great surprise she saw there was a metal box, the end of which protruded slightly from the rock shelf on which it rested. The cave widened on that side, making an alcove which was out of sight of the entrance.

She took down the box. It was fairly heavy. She placed it on the sand away from the alcove where the light from the cave entrance fell dimly upon it. There was no lock, and when she pulled at the lid it opened easily as if used often. She gasped. There, carefully packed, were ear-rings, necklaces and other pieces of jewellery. A bag lay to one side of the box.

She gazed at the jewellery. Had these things been stolen? She lifted the bag, felt its bulk and weight, heard the chink of coin. Was her money among its contents? Or the remainder of it?

Her thoughts raced on. Who had placed the jewellery and money in the casket?

Memories, voices, faces crowded her mind. The man and woman below her window the night before. Jane's hostility...

Ruperta's thoughts returned to the present. Suppose someone came now and found her with the open casket, she could be in danger! Hastily she closed the lid and placed the casket back on its shelf.

As she made her way along the path, it occurred to her that she must have left footprints in the cave. But they could not be very distinct, and the next tide would remove them, she told herself.

On regaining the house she managed to reach her bedroom without anyone seeing her. No doubt her mother was still busy in the kitchen, and John at whatever work he did. Once inside her room she realised that someone had been in it since she had left it earlier that morning. A mirror had been placed on the window sill against one of the mullions, there were candles; more bedclothes had been laid on the bed.

She smiled to herself and guessed that her mother had been at work here...

Hastily Ruperta tidied her hair and went downstairs. She found her mother alone in the kitchen, thanked her for the mirror, candles and extra bedclothes, and men-

74

tioned the cave she had found.

As they talked Ruperta became convinced that her mother knew nothing about the box in the cave...

Later that afternoon Ruperta with her mother joined Sir Peter in the parlour. It was cosy, small and comfortable. Sir Peter, who had been dozing in front of the fire, appeared to welcome the two women's company, and upheld the conversation most of the time, asking Ruperta about the latest London news and rumours.

After some time Ann Colston went back to the kitchen. When she had gone, Sir Peter said: 'It has been so pleasant to talk to you. I am for the most part glum and full of misgivings. The truth is,' he went on, 'we are poor. Since the King's return, we are no better than we were under Cromwell. Once we were a proud family. Now we are forced to do any work we can get.'

Just then Ruperta caught sight of two riders approaching, and recognised them as Jane Colston and her father. She wondered how Jane in particular would react to the news of her staying on until tomorrow...

At supper that evening John ate seriously and steadily, avoiding all attempts to engage him in conversation.

Jane said with irritated coldness: 'I thought, Mistress Wittel, that this day you were to journey on to Chodbury.'

Before Ruperta could speak, her mother said quickly: 'I thought, Jane, that our guest would benefit from another night's rest before leaving. Besides, it has rained nearly all day. It has been no weather for travelling.'

Jane lapsed into silence, eyeing Ruperta across the table with sullen antagonism.

She was glad when the meal was over, and Jane and John left the table together. Sir Peter and his son-in-law went to the parlour, and Ruperta had her mother to herself for a satisfyingly long time...

On leaving the kitchen Ruperta crossed the hall towards the stairs, meaning to go up to her room. Only a candle on the great table and the sinking fire on the hearth gave some light. She became aware of a voice coming from the direction of the porch. Ruperta recognised it immediately – Jane Colston's.

Ruperta caught a few words.

'You heard ... another night ... must be a spy, an informer ... trap you ... you must ... feared ... happen.'

Ruperta started up the stairs, in no doubt

that she was the 'spy' of whom Jane spoke. But who was she talking to?

Ruperta stumbled, banging her shoe against a step. She was conscious of the porch door opening, footsteps in the hall.

A moment of unreasoning fear caught her. The stairs seemed endless. Would she ever reach the top? She tried to will herself not to turn round, but failed. Glanced back. In the shadows she discerned a figure, its blur of a face watching her. Ruperta forced herself to walk slowly, naturally, along the dark gallery, though she wanted to run, gain her bedroom quickly.

She pushed her door open, then felt for the bolt in the darkness, but could not, in her haste, find it. She hurried over to the window, stood with her back to the mirror, heart beating fast. Why was she behaving in such a fashion?

She told herself to calm down; and then later she would open the door, walk along the gallery, down into the hall, pretending that she had heard nothing.

But was she not in some danger now? Jane and whoever had been in the porch with her must have realised that something of the conversation had been overheard. Ruperta shivered. Was that a shape in the beams above her? Imagination was tormenting her. When she did go upstairs, she must remember to take a candle and light it, before she returned to the bedroom again.

Beyond the windows the wind was strong enough to cover the sound of footsteps approaching, but she could see the line of light below the door grow brighter. A knock startled her, made her gasp. She edged away quickly from the windows, pressed against the wall alongside. The knock came again, quickly, firmly. When she tried to call out, she found that her throat had dried up.

The door opened. A face floated above a single candle, and she recognised John Colston. The light reached dimly to the windows, and Ruperta saw his gaze rest upon her. Shame and pride overcame her fear; she straightened and moved nearer to the window again.

For a long moment they stared at each other.

'Mistress Wittel, I...'

She did not hear John out, courtesy forgotten in the stress. Her voice came out as a croak. 'I was just fetching a candle.'

He took a step inside the door and halted. 'I have a candle here. You can light yours from it.'

A sudden fury erupted in Ruperta. She hated the thought that this man had caught her cringing in the dark; and all her recent suspicions she now guessed to be well founded.

'And have you brought the rest of the money and the ring that you robbed me of?' she flung at him. 'The highwayman that night – I know now it was you.'

Apart from a slight widening of the eyes, his expression did not change under her accusation. 'No, I did not rob you,' he said calmly.

'You deny it?' Her words tumbled out. 'I found money, jewellery in a cave...'

He nodded. 'I saw the footprints.'

She shook her head in bewilderment. 'You would lie when the proceeds of your robberies are there?'

There was a glint of anger in his eyes. 'I did not stop you on the road.'

'B-but – but, I heard your sister...'

'She is anxious when strangers come.' He gave a dismissive wave of his hand.

But Ruperta was not to be put off. 'Do you deny that the box is yours?' she persisted.

'Valuables have to be kept somewhere safe,' he pointed out.

'That box contains women's jewellery as well as money,' she said. 'But perhaps you wear necklaces?'

For a moment Ruperta thought she had gone too far, and he was going to strike her. After a moment he cried: 'I told the truth. I did not rob you.'

It flashed into Ruperta's mind that she had not recognised any of the valuables as having been taken from her two companions on the coach. Her ring had not been there either.

'You did not rob me, then,' she said. 'But what of other occasions?'

His silence and expression replied for him. Ruperta was shocked. Her half-brother a highway robber! 'But why?' she asked in a whisper.

John Colston made sure the door was shut, then came farther into the room. 'Why d'you want to know? You're a stranger. What interest have you in me?'

Ruperta wished she could tell him. 'Remember,' she said, 'that I was frightened to death by one of your kind, my valuables were stolen and my journey spoilt. What makes men like you rob and frighten people who have done you no harm?'

He stood scrutinising her closely, and then

began to speak in low, angry tones. 'When I go out at night – and it is not often – it is for this family, my family. My grandfather was Sir John Colston, owner of Colston Hall, about a mile to the north. He was killed at Marston Moor, fighting for the King. My father fought for him as well. When the King's cause was lost, my father was forced to sell his house and lands to pay the fine he had incurred by backing the wrong side.'

And so the Colstons, Ruperta said to herself, had to live at Ravall's Court with Sir Peter.

John went on: 'Colston Hall is my father's home. It and the land should be restored to him by the present King. But he does nothing for us.'

Ruperta knew this problem was a sore one in many families. If Colston Hall had been confiscated, the family might have got it back. In cases of sale, however, injustices were bound to arise. It would have been difficult to find a way of returning the property and lands without complicated and almost impossible legal difficulties arising.

'Who lives at Colston Hall now?' Ruperta asked. The eyes above the candlelight burned more fiercely into hers.

'It was bought by a family we knew well.

You have seen how hard my mother works. She went grey long before her time. She seldom complains, but I know how she feels. Sudworth Hall – as they call it now – is always in her mind.'

Sudworth. The name evoked a memory in Ruperta. 'Was that young, fair-haired man who called this morning from there?'

'That's the one. The place belongs to him now. His father died last year; his mother had been dead for some time.'

So it was the master of Sudworth Hall who had kissed her, Ruperta thought…

John Colston asked in the same harsh, embittered tones: 'Do you know where my father and sister have been all this day?'

Ruperta shook her head silently.

'My father often works as a gardener and my sister in the kitchen at the Hall. Yet that place is ours by rights. They bring in a pittance for their labour, but it helps us to continue living here.'

He must have observed the question in her eyes. 'As for me, during the day I look after the few sheep we have, or work on our few remaining acres.' Then with grim determination and a tinge of satisfaction in his voice, he said: 'Some day I shall have enough money, then my father and Jane will not have to work up there any more. We shall be independent again.'

Ruperta could guess at the humiliation he must feel for his father and sister. She regarded him with more understanding and some sympathy, and now realised why her arrival at the house had upset Jane.

He said abruptly: 'What I came to tell you was that I have arranged for the return of the coach horse to its owners.'

'Thank you,' Ruperta said. 'I am afraid I forgot all about it.'

He leaned forward and lit the candle for her; the extra light duplicated in the mirror, brightening the room. The tension between them had eased, and the bitter anger had drained away from him, taking the tautness from his expression, though he still looked tired. Ruperta was not surprised. His night rides, infrequent though they might be, were obviously a severe strain.

Suddenly he asked: 'Are you a spy or an informer?' His tone suggested that it mattered nothing to him whether she was or not.

'I am neither,' she retorted strongly. 'I am a traveller, or was, on the highway, minding my own affairs.'

'My sister thinks you are. I do not, though I would not put it beyond some men to use a woman to trap the likes of me.' He eyed her thoughtfully for a few seconds, then asked: 'What will you do now? Denounce me to the authorities as soon as you leave here? Do you think you ought to do that?'

Ruperta gave a rapid and definite shake of her head, conscious of his continuing and close scrutiny of her. 'No, I shall go on my way. I want to forget about highwaymen.' Even as she spoke, new and strange ideas were entering her mind. 'Besides,' she went on, 'I would not bring more worry to this house. It will come soon enough if you continue on your dangerous course.'

She saw his shoulders move in a tiny shrug. 'I'm also mindful of your family's kindness to me, Mr Colston.'

'You have been in the house long enough to call me John. All I ask is that when you leave, you forget my name, and where I live. My parents and grandfather know nothing of my activities by night. But Jane guessed, and I was forced to take her into my confidence.'

'I shall not betray you,' she said. 'And my name is Ruperta.' She hoped that Jane had not told him about the other name – Elizabeth.

'Ruperta,' he repeated. 'Your father must

84

have been a most fervent Royalist.'

She nodded, smiling inwardly. Her father certainly had been, and continued to be.

John's face relaxed. He seemed to have accepted her assurance that she would keep his secret. There was a short silence between them, the wind moaned outside, and the candle flames fluttered in the draught.

John said slowly: 'My mother thinks more of Father than of herself.' His face became fierce, hard again. 'Soon I shall see that my father has enough money to buy her beautiful clothes, before she's too old to enjoy them.'

Ruperta saw his free hand clench tightly. Then he went on: 'And Jane grows impatient to dress as a lady: I fear she is in love with Roger Sudworth and would like him to pay her some attention. So you see, Ruperta, I am obliged to go hunting at night.'

With a feeling of sadness Ruperta looked at him. A kindly and obviously devoted son, well-meaning and with good intentions, dreaming a dream that would not come true...

'Why do you concern yourself about me?' he asked her.

She burst out: 'Why throw your life away? You will bring sorrow and disgrace upon your family – the very people you want to help – if you are caught.'

John's gaze slid slowly from her face, and he half turned away, but not before she had seen his change of expression. Her point had gone home, she was certain.

He moved away towards the door, looked at her very seriously and said: 'I know, Ruperta, but I need the money.' With that he was gone...

Ruperta went early to bed. But not to sleep, only to wrestle with the thoughts and questions battering at her mind after her conversation with John Colston.

Could she leave the house without doing something to help what was after all her new-found family? She might stay for a few days and decide what was to be done. She could sell some of her own possessions. Her father was generous, and at home she had quite a lot of money. But what could she do about John? He was set on getting money in his own way. She sighed in the darkness at the confusion of her thoughts.

Would it not be better if she just disappeared out of their lives as suddenly as she had arrived?

It was late by the time she had decided that this was to be her course of action, and she fell fast asleep…

Not surprisingly it was far from early when she woke up. She washed and dressed quickly, then made her way downstairs to say good-bye. There was no one about, so she approached the kitchen, sure that that was where she would find her mother.

Ann Colston was slumped at the table, head in hands, dejection in every line of her body. At Ruperta's entry she straightened, drawing a hand across each eye quickly as she did so.

It was at that moment that Ruperta changed her mind, knew that she could not leave. She would stay on and try to help in some way. 'I have decided, Mother,' she said hurriedly, 'to stay on for a while and help you, if you are willing to have me. I will bake, clean, anything.' She smiled cheerfully. 'What do you say?'

Ann Colston shook her head, but her face had brightened. 'Your offer is a very kindly one. Already I feel you are one of my family – which you are. But I cannot keep you here, in a strange house. And I fear it is a far from pleasant one at present.'

'I have two weeks to spare. Please let me stay,' Ruperta said, and put an arm about the bowed shoulders…

So Ruperta's self-imposed employment at Ravall's Court began the next day, and with it came a surprise. She was upstairs in the gallery cleaning the windows, and had heard someone arrive. Her mother greeted the visitor with a little cry of pleasure. There was some talk, which Ruperta did not catch, and then Jane came upstairs. It seemed that she would not be going to Sudworth Hall today, but Ruperta did not feel she could ask about it.

'Mr Sudworth is here, and would like to speak with you,' Jane said in tones of cold dislike.

'Mr Sudworth?' exclaimed Ruperta in amazement. Jane's back was already turned, and Ruperta stared after her. What on earth could he want? She glanced down at herself and gasped. She was scarcely looking her best. Hurrying into her room, she tidied herself and arranged her hair quickly in front of the mirror. She remembered how curt and unfriendly Jane had sounded, and linked that with John's suspicion that his sister was in love with Roger. Could she be jealous?

CHAPTER FOUR

Roger Sudworth was standing with his back to the hearth, looking straight in front of him. As she came out of her room and saw him, Ruperta was conscious that for all his elegance there was a sturdy quality about him – like an oak, she thought confusedly.

A step creaked, and he looked up sharply, his face relaxing into a smile as he watched her descend. There was no sign of Jane or her mother. They had presumably retired to allow the visitor to speak privately with Ruperta.

She stood uncertainly at the foot of the staircase, and he came up to her, smiling pleasantly.

'Good morning, Mistress Wittel. You will pardon this visit so soon after my last. I assure you I shall not behave like this again–' his eyes twinkled– 'for another day at least.'

Ruperta's answering smile was broad. She could not stop herself.

'And what have you been doing since I last saw you?' he asked.

'Mrs Colston has much to do,' she said. 'I have been doing what I can to help.' Quite suddenly she was regretting that she was still in the dress she had been wearing at their last meeting. Why had he come back so soon?

He regarded her steadily for a few moments, then glanced towards the kitchen, before speaking in lowered tones. 'I have important news for you. I cannot acquaint you with it here. Will you accompany me a short distance from the house?'

Surprised and somewhat disturbed, Ruperta hesitated.

'I can assure you I shall not carry you off, whatever you may think of my past behaviour,' he said.

She wondered what he had to say, and why it could not be said in the house...

'Please, Mistress Wittel, we shall not be long. It is very much to your advantage to hear what I have to say,' he told her.

She made up her mind. 'Very well, though I shall have to tell Mrs Colston that I am going out with you.'

He smiled and gave a nod which was almost a bow. 'You will be quite safe.'

Ruperta made for the kitchen. Jane turned away from the fire, her hostile gaze meeting Ruperta's.

She wondered if it were wise for her to speak in front of Jane. If she were jealous, as she appeared to be, the knowledge that Ruperta was to go off with Roger Sudworth would make maters worse, but short of asking to speak with her mother privately, there was nothing she could do.

So Ruperta told her mother of the visitor's request, adding: 'I'm sure I shall not be away for long, though I cannot tell why he should want me to accompany him.'

'Did he not say where?' Jane's voice was sharp, accusing.

Ruperta glanced at her, and shook her head.

Mrs Colston looked bewildered. 'I cannot understand his coming yesterday and now today. It is years since he was last in this house.' Then with regret she went on: 'They were such friends, he and John, but John has taken a dislike to him. It should not be. It is foolish of him.' Her face brightened. 'But off you go, Ruperta. I must not burden you with that affair.'

Leaving them, Ruperta hurried upstairs to fetch her cloak, then joined Roger Sudworth outside. He was waiting with two horses.

'I have brought you a mount,' he said.

'I had not realised, Mr Sudworth, that the

91

short distance would need a horse,' she said with some apprehension.

'Trust me, Mistress Wittel. What I have to say cannot be said anywhere near this house.'

She studied him a moment. There was nothing to fear, she told herself. He was well known to the family, and in any case she was curious to hear what he had to say to her. She allowed him to help her up into the saddle. When she was settled he mounted, and they set off.

Ruperta glanced back at the house. Framed in a window, watching, was Jane Colston, a set look on her face. Ruperta was glad when they were through the arched gateway and her back was to the house.

They rode at a walking pace. Her companion did not speak, and for the most part looked straight ahead, but she was aware of his occasional glances sideways at her. She in her turn observed that he was looking very serious, though he smiled whenever their eyes met.

When they had gone some distance she could not contain her curiosity any longer.

'Mr Sudworth,' she said firmly, 'where are you taking me?' She was not alarmed, but thought it was time he told her more.

'A woman's curiosity,' he replied mockingly, shaking his head at her. 'Be patient, Mistress Wittel. Not long now.'

Ruperta looked back. She could just see the dark mass of trees almost screening Ravall's Court, and had a sense of comfort from knowing that it was still within sight. They were entering a wood now, the undergrowth thick, the sky a patchy grey above. Something in Ruperta's mind stirred, trying to make her remember... She felt that she was on the verge of some discovery...

She became aware that Roger Sudworth was now paying careful attention to their surroundings, looking about him as he rode. It was gloomy, the green a darker green, the tree-trunks black towers, against which her companion's hair gleamed golden. The path narrowed sharply, and after a few more yards Roger Sudworth stopped and sat still, listening. They heard only the scurrying of some small animal in the undergrowth, a flutter of a bird above, the jingle of a bit. A leaf drifted down, touching branches on the way.

Evidently satisfied that all was well, the young man dismounted.

Ruperta was now mildly alarmed. They were out of sight of the house, and she was alone with a man she had met for the first time only the day before.

He looked up at her, guessing her thoughts. 'Don't be afraid, this is as far as we are going.'

Nevertheless, she was uneasy as she watched him look about him warily, and then approach a large tree some five yards away, his feet crunching on the fallen leaves. Reaching it, she saw him bend over at its base and begin throwing grass and twigs aside.

Then, to her utter surprise, he picked up two objects, one in each hand, and returned with them, dropping them on the ground at the side of her horse.

'Your property, I believe.' He looked up at her, a smile in the vivid blue eyes suggesting that he was enjoying her amazement.

She stared mutely at the two bags, and was hardly conscious of his helping her down. They were hers, no doubt about that. They were the bags that she had last seen strapped to the top of the coach with those of her fellow travellers. 'H-how…' She halted, unable to get the words out.

He smiled gently. 'You told me what had befallen you. The road is not far from here. I looked along it, found the coach, and retrieved your bags from it,' he explained simply.

She did not understand. 'But – but how did you know which were mine? They were not marked.' Again she had the feeling that she was about to discover something.

Roger Sudworth knocked the dirt from his hands before answering. 'They were the only ones left, Mistress Wittel. Wonderful that they remained there, what with the rogues who prey upon that stretch of road!'

He picked up one bag, swung it up behind his saddle, then bent for the other and proceeded to fasten them both.

She was just about to thank him when he said over his shoulder: 'How is your head? You are completely recovered now, I hope?'

'My head? Oh, I had forgotten.' She smiled. 'I was not seriously hurt.'

The moment the words were out of her mouth, certain facts came together in her mind. Roger Sudworth should not have known about the pain in her head ... the way he sat his horse ... riding with him ... she had done that before ... he was the highwayman who had robbed her...

Ruperta's instincts allowed only one solution. She turned and ran towards the house a mile away. She tripped over an age-old root and sprawled clumsily on the ground. When she attempted to scramble upright, firm hands turned her and held her down. Struggling and writhing she tried to break free from the man kneeling beside her. At last she lay still, gasping for breath from her exertions and from the fury within her.

'Is that the way you show your gratitude for the return of your lost possessions?' Roger Sudworth looked at her, his voice amused, but his eyes heavy with emotion.

Ruperta's fury erupted into fierce speech. She glared up savagely at him. 'You thief! You stopped the coach! You robbed me!' she flung at him.

Apart from a slight widening of the eyes, his expression did not change. 'Why did you run, Mistress Ruperta? I am trying to return...'

'You did return some of my money,' she cut in. 'And you found my baggage on the abandoned coach. How grateful must I be for that – and for the fact that you are hurting my wrists?'

He released his grip slightly. She struggled to rise. 'Let me at least sit up,' she snapped.

'I want your word of honour that you will cease to struggle, and will not try to run away again.'

'What do you – a common thief – know about honour?' she cried.

'Your word,' he said calmly and firmly.

She nodded, accepting defeat. He helped her to sit up, and knelt on one knee at her side. 'Give me your hand, please.'

She made no movement, her eyes hostile and suspicious.

'Please.' His voice was like a pistol shot in the quietness. A command, not a request, his eyes flashing blue fire.

Cautiously she put out her right hand. He took hold of it and then, to her astonishment he slid the ring, which she had thought lost for ever, on to her finger.

'You see, there was no need for alarm,' he said and laughed.

'I was shocked and frightened. Would you not expect that?' she said, twisting the ring on her finger. Then she cried, still angry: 'Is England full of highwaymen?'

Roger Sudworth looked faintly surprised. 'You have been unfortunate once through me. Have you been stopped on the road before?'

She shook her head, inspected her ring. She must not betray John Colston. When she looked up again, she found that her companion's gaze was still fixed on her.

There was a glint of amusement in his eyes, which irritated her.

'Are you not going to thank me?' he asked.

'Thank you for returning what you stole from me? You should live by honesty.'

His amusement gave place to anger. 'What do you know of honesty? By the looks of you, you've led an easy life. How could you know of the choice to be made between what you call honesty and a sense of obligation?'

'There is no excuse for frightening and robbing people,' hissed Ruperta in a new upsurge of fury. 'Why did you do it? You surely are not poor? You have a house and land, fine clothes…'

Roger Sudworth stood up quickly, strode over to his horse, his face set. Her words had evidently stung him. ''Tis a long story, and of no interest to you, Mistress Wittel.'

Scrambling to her feet, she followed him. 'I think it is,' she retorted sharply, 'and the more so because I was one of those you picked on to further whatever cause you campaign for.'

He swung round to face her, his expression quite changed. Smiling, he said: 'Do you remember our conversation yesterday? About what made a man go out on the road?' He spread his arms. 'Well, for me it's the sport, the challenge, the gamble.'

Ruperta shook her head incredulously. 'I cannot believe you. There must be something more.'

There had been something false about his sudden cheerfulness. It was almost as if he had put on a mask...

He told her: 'I have but one quarrel with the business. I cannot distinguish between the good people and the bad until I have stopped the coach.' Here he grinned at her. 'Nor can I tell whether there will be a beautiful woman on it.' He paused, then went on: 'I dislike having to take from certain people.'

She looked at him dubiously, softening somewhat. A plausible and engaging rogue! 'As in my own case,' she said.

He nodded at her finger. 'I have returned some of what I took,' he reminded her.

'So you did. It is to your credit,' she admitted, though a little grudgingly. He must still have the rest of the money he had taken from her. But she was most thankful to get the ring back. It was valuable, not only in terms of money, but for what it meant to her as a gift from her father.

What a world away her London home seemed now, contrasting with her present

99

position, conversing with a highwayman in a wood in a remote part of England! And even more strange was the fact that she knew another young gentleman of the road – her half-brother.

She brushed leaves and grass from her clothes, then walked towards her mount. 'Now will you take me back, Mr Sudworth?' she said rather stiffly.

'That is my immediate intention.' He gave a little bow, solemn-faced, but his eyes smiled into hers. She accepted his offer to help her mount, and they set off.

For a while she avoided his glances, but then it became difficult for her to maintain a dignified silence. She wanted to ask questions but she could not, if she persisted in trying to keep on her dignity. She smiled inwardly, deploring the fact that she had shown little of that quality during the last few minutes. And the man riding alongside did deserve some gratitude. After all he had had no need to recover her baggage or to return her ring.

At one and the same time he fascinated and annoyed her...

'A gold coin for your thoughts, Mistress Wittel.'

She glanced across at him, glad of the

interruption, but unable to stop herself retorting: 'Perhaps it would be one of my own, Mr Sudworth.'

He smiled ruefully at her. 'You will not forgive me easily, will you?'

He was hardly likely to provide answers to her questions if she did not behave a little more pleasantly towards him. She flashed him an apologetic smile. 'You have done me a service for which I am thankful. As for my thoughts, I cannot rid myself of a most puzzling one.'

'Then I must do all I can to give you an answer so that you will think even better of me.'

'Why did you take me with you that night, and not one of the others?'

Roger Sudworth gave a chuckle. 'Because a gentleman of the road becomes lonely – and I did not fancy the company of either of your fellow passengers.'

For that matter, she had not much cared for the two men herself...

Roger went on: 'I felt sorry for you. You looked frightened, unprotected.' His expression changed to one of admiration. 'Yet the way you spoke to me – it was very courageous, though not everything you said was in my favour. Never have I met such a woman.

You flare up like gunpowder.'

'Perhaps with good reason,' she returned, unable to restrain a smile. She still could not believe that he played such a dangerous game as highway robbery for love of excitement. There must be some other reason.

He stopped his horse and pointed ahead. 'Do you remember the light in the window that night?'

She nodded.

'This is almost where we were then,' he informed her. The dark outline of Ravall's Court behind its trees could be seen.

They moved on and Ruperta was surprised at herself for feeling a pang of regret that they would be back at the house before long. She wanted to know more about the man riding with her. He was a yard or two ahead of her, and she observed his preoccupied look.

'Mr Sudworth...' she began.

He looked round at her and smiled. 'Well?'

'How long have you been a highwayman?'

'About a year. Why do you ask? Do you think my apprenticeship not finished yet?'

He seemed to think the matter a joke. How could he? She tried to match his carefree tones, but failed. 'Your apprenticeship must have been a thorough one, seeing that you have survived so long. It is said that even the best do not last much longer than a year.'

He shrugged. 'Then I shall have done what I had to do. The risk adds spice to the game.'

'Are you going out tonight?' she asked tremulously.

He studied her face carefully before answering. 'Can a woman keep a secret? I shall run a bigger risk if I tell you.'

'What you have told me and let me see already would be enough,' Ruperta retorted in some annoyance at his unwillingness to trust her further.

He nodded in agreement. 'Yes, it is so. You must have some witch's power over me. No one knows as much as you do about my business.' He sighed in mock regret. 'Now a woman holds my life in her hands.'

'I shall not betray you,' she said. 'But I wish that you would not persist in going out at night.'

After a long silence he said: 'I play the game only when I know it is going to be worth while.' He turned in the saddle to look fully at her. 'I have information that there will be rich people on the coach from Chodbury tomorrow.'

She was aware of rising exasperation tinged with fear. 'You'll be caught sooner or later.' She had been frightened of Roger Sudworth when he had held up the coach, and again not so many minutes ago in the wood. Now she was afraid for him.

He studied her with a slightly puzzled expression. 'Why concern yourself about me? If my turn comes, it will be one the fewer. And no doubt some at Ravall's Court will clap their hands.'

Ruperta was to think about that bitter statement later. 'But why throw your life away?' she cried. 'The odds are against you now, 'tis only a matter of time. Leave it while you can.'

'My thanks for your kindly thoughts, but I think good fortune will ride with me yet awhile. It is to be hoped so, for my business is not finished. I set myself a task...'

Suddenly the blue eyes were on her, his manner swiftly changed again. 'But unfortunately, dear Mistress Wittel, the sport pulls upon me too much.'

Ruperta refused to believe it. He had said that he had set himself a task. Why – or on behalf of whom?

He grinned at her. 'But it does my heart good to know of your concern for me.'

She looked away. There was nothing she could do if he persisted in his dangerous game, whatever the reason. She might as well change the subject.

'I have, as you know, Mr Sudworth, not been long at Ravall's Court, but it has been made plain to me that you are not over welcome there,' she said. 'Yet you and John Colston used to be great friends – or so I understand.'

Roger Sudworth gazed ahead as he spoke. 'He has still my friendship if he will see beyond his dreams. As boys we were so close that we might have been brothers. But gradually we grew apart. He seemed to resent my living at Sudworth Hall – I sometimes wish that my father had not renamed it.

'But it was not his fault that the Colstons were ruined by the Civil War. John will not admit that my family had any troubles at all. I am not as rich as he makes himself believe; I cannot be as generous as I would wish. Jeremy Colston has accepted the situation, though it is he who has most reason to feel bitter. You may have heard that my father found work for Jeremy Colston and Jane. But for that they might have starved. They are not in such desperate need now, but to some extent they still depend on what I pay them.'

Perhaps, Ruperta thought, Roger had taken to highway robbery in order to keep Sudworth Hall going...

'You must allow me to show you the Hall some day soon,' Roger said in more cheerful tones. 'When are you leaving Ravall's Court?'

'In a few days, I suppose.' She was not able to keep a note of regret out of her voice.

'Then, if you agree,' he said, 'I shall call for you on Friday in the afternoon, Mistress Wittel, and I promise to escort you back to Ravall's Court afterwards.'

He stopped his horse, swinging round to face her. 'I like the name Ruperta. May I call you that?'

Ruperta extended her hand. 'Then Ruperta I am to you.'

He took her hand. 'And you must call me Roger,' he said.

She smiled her agreement.

His gaze seemed to encompass her and isolate her from the world. A mischievous gleam appeared in his eyes. 'In the short time we have known each other, we have done a great deal of quarrelling. I do not wish to risk another angry scene, but I must.'

She stared at him, not knowing whether to

smile or be solemn. What was so important that he had to risk incurring her displeasure again?

'D'you remember, not many minutes ago,' he said, 'you warned me against carrying on with my nightly business?'

'Yes, I do.' What on earth was coming?

'I cannot have much time left.' His voice dropped perceptibly, became almost serious, though his eyes still held amusement. 'That being so,' he went on, 'I must ask favours quickly, otherwise I shall leave matters undone.'

He took off his hat and leaned over towards her. 'Robber, thief I may be, but this time I shall not steal. I beg of you a kiss, Ruperta.'

Ruperta's features dissolved into a happy smile tinged with relief. Impulsively she touched his arm. 'There will be no quarrel over that,' she murmured.

Their lips met. His mouth was warm and demanding. The kiss lasted for seconds only, but days could have turned to night for Ruperta.

She drew away. Two meetings. Two kisses. Had she made it all too easy for him? 'I must return, Roger,' she muttered. Her lips had told him more about her feelings, she guessed, than she had intended them to.

'Otherwise they will think I have kidnapped you.' His voice had thickened, and she had never seen him look so serious.

'Leave night business alone, Roger.' The words were out before she realised she had said them.

He glanced at her and away. She could tell from his expression that he would take no notice of her pleading. The smiling mask was on his face again.

'You will keep my secret, Ruperta?'

She nodded, wondering sadly how long that would be necessary. He was not to be dissuaded, that was that. She looked at the house again. Had their kiss been seen?

They started off again, Roger leading. Ruperta saw that someone on horseback was standing under the arch. Drawing nearer she recognised John Colston.

Roger greeted him pleasantly, but John barred the way in and said: 'You are not coming any farther, Sudworth.'

'I have retrieved Mistress Wittel's baggage. I would like to set it down for her at the house,' Roger said evenly.

'I can do that. I could have done the whole thing, if I'd been asked.' John glanced accusingly at Ruperta.

'I thought you would be busy – I did not wish to trouble you,' she protested.

Her half-brother's lips were a thin slit as his eyes returned to the other man. 'It is true that Sudworth always has time to spare,' he said.

The two former friends eyed each other tensely. Ruperta did not want trouble between them, especially over herself.

Roger's pleasant expression did not alter, but his voice was hard as he said: 'I have no wish to come in, John. Only to deliver Mistress Wittel and her baggage.'

'Let us get this clear,' John said. 'I am no longer John to you. I call you Sudworth, and you call me Colston.'

This was too much for Ruperta.

'Mr Colston,' she said rather stiffly, 'I have no wish to interfere. You have been kind to me, but so has Mr Sudworth. He has put himself about to help me. Please allow him to pass.'

Roger waved a hand. 'Mistress Wittel, I see this affair upsets you. I shall leave you, though not without misgivings, to this mannerless oaf.' Then he swept off his hat to Ruperta. 'Good day, Mistress Wittel. We shall be meeting again.'

Suddenly all was confusion. John drove his

horse at his former friend.

'No! John! Roger!' Ruperta cried out in appeal and warning.

Roger swung his mount away as John tried clumsily to pull him from the saddle. Rupert hoped that Roger would have the good sense to ride off and stay away until John had come to his senses, but he merely avoided John's attempts to unseat him, recovering quickly from the initial shock of the sudden attack. No words were uttered in the intensity of the situation, only gasps of effort and the sound of hoofs scraping and slithering on the stones, the chink and jingle of the bridles.

Roger was at a disadvantage, Ruperta saw with alarm. Her baggage made it hard for his horse to turn quickly. Fortunately his horse was a better one than John's rather clumsy mount. If it had not been so alarming, it would have been a ridiculous sight – the two horses sliding about, one moment head to head, the next head to tail as the riders jockeyed for position.

Under the stress of John's attack, Roger lost his temper. Instead of merely fending off his opponent, he fisted him away, rocking him in the saddle and once almost lifting him from it.

Ruperta prayed that neither man would be harmed. Her life had become entangled with theirs. Each occupied a special place in her thoughts – her half-brother, John, and Roger, who in a short time had captured her interest and perhaps even her heart.

Roger suddenly retreated several yards. Then he drove his horse forward again, catching John temporarily off balance. John's horse reared up near the side of the arched entrance. He was thrown off backwards, striking his head against the stonework. He fell to the ground and lay still.

Ruperta, dumb with shock, slid from her horse and dashed towards his crumpled figure. But Roger was quicker still, crouching at John's side and looking acutely anxious. She heard him muttering vehemently: 'You fool, you fool, my friend! What have I done?'

Ruperta saw the closed eyes, the pale face. 'Is he...?'

Roger shook his head, searching John's face. 'Stunned, I think. Will you help me to lift him?'

With some assistance from Ruperta, Roger got John into his arms. 'I'll carry him inside,' he said. 'Will you go ahead and tell them to have his bed ready? And say that he fell from his horse. There is no point in distressing his family by telling the truth.'

She nodded, picked up her skirts and dashed ahead. Roger following with John like a baby in his arms.

Jane came out of the porch and rushed past Ruperta without a word. How much had she seen?

Roger said something reassuring to her as she bent over her brother, and Ruperta went into the house, found her mother, and gave her Roger's version of what had happened.

She turned very white when she saw her son, and it was Jane who led the way up the stairs, Roger trying to comfort Mrs Colston as they followed.

Ruperta waited at the foot of the stairs, hoping desperately that John's injury was not serious, and that he would recover quickly. She sighed. What a morning it had been! Shocks, kisses and violence. So much had happened.

A few minutes later Roger came down, smiling. 'The madman is recovering,' he said. 'I'd best be going before he tries again. Never did I think that he could behave like that.' He did look bewildered, and Ruperta heard the hurt in his voice.

'Are you quite unharmed?' she asked.

'I am, thanks to you, Ruperta. Your warning was timely.' A flash of humour appeared in his face. 'You are indeed a lucky woman for me. If you were to ride behind me on the road I should always feel safe.'

She shivered. 'Do not speak of it!'

Suddenly he thought of something. 'And I forgot your baggage!' he exclaimed. 'I hope the horses have not gone far.'

With that he left her in some haste, to reappear after a few minutes with only one horse – his own.

She was relieved to see her baggage which he brought in and deposited by the fireplace. 'Your horse has gone, Ruperta. It is of no consequence,' he said, 'for it will probably make for the stables.' He took her hand. 'You have not forgotten, in all this trouble, about our next meeting?'

She gave a little shake of her head, and his next words echoed her thoughts. 'It is to be hoped that it will be a more peaceful one than this morning's.'

'Will you call here?' she asked with trepidation.

'I will not antagonise John further, but only because of his family. I shall be waiting near the gateway just after noon,' Roger told her. He must have seen other fears in her face. 'What is the matter, Ruperta?'

She spoke in a whisper, and he bent to hear. 'W-when are you going on the road again?'

'Tonight. And tomorrow.'

'Oh!' She would have to worry and wait. 'Could you,' she went on, 'let me know that you are safe afterwards? If I waited at my window, would you give me some sign?'

His face came alive with pleasure. 'So you care for me a little!' He bowed. 'Your wish is my command – it shall be done. As soon as I have relieved a certain personage of his ill-gotten possessions, then I shall find some means of informing you that I am safe and well.'

An uneasy feeling came over Ruperta at his words, and she tried to quell it. How could he be so light-hearted, so contemptuous of the dangers surrounding him?

She saw him glance past her, his lips forming a thin, polite smile. And Ruperta turned just in time to see Jane's face visible above the gallery rail, hear her footsteps as she began to descend the stairs. Had she overheard some of their conversation?

'I must go now, Ruperta,' said Roger quickly. He half turned away, then evidently bethought himself of something. 'Quickly, which is your bedroom?' he whispered.

Ruperta stared at him blankly. The man was full of surprises.

'I mean – how may I know it from outside?' he said impatiently.

'The end one at the front – nearest the stable,' she said, sorry that she had misjudged him.

'Not good-bye.' His lips formed the words, and he left her, with Jane hurrying after him and paying no attention to Ruperta.

She heard their voices fading away outside. But whatever was said between them did not take long, for Jane reappeared almost immediately. The glance that she gave Ruperta as she made her way toward the stairs again, contained one emotion – hate, so powerful that Ruperta almost felt as if it had been a blow.

CHAPTER FIVE

During the remainder of the day, Ruperta avoided her half-sister and busied herself helping her mother and freeing her to attend to the welfare of John, who was recovering from his head injury, but complaining of pain in his right arm.

It was with some surprise that after dark Ruperta found John in the hall, staring morosely into the fire, and disdaining the company of the others in the parlour. She found it hard to feel much sympathy for him, and longed to scold him for his attempt to harm his former friend, but decided not to risk upsetting him further. After all, she was supposed to be a stranger with no connection with the family, and too much concern on her part might lead to awkward questions.

His eyes flicked upwards and down again as she pulled up a chair and seated herself. 'How are you feeling now, John?' she asked gently.

'My arm hurts. I have difficulty in moving it.'

'I'm sorry,' she murmured, but she felt relieved. As long as he had difficulty in using the limb, he could hardly go out and commit highway robbery. It was, perhaps, a blessing in disguise for him.

'Why did you attack Roger?' she asked. 'You could have killed him.'

At first she thought he was going to ignore her. Then she saw his face beginning to darken.

'I never meant to do that!' he exclaimed fiercely. He went on in bitter hopelessness: 'I've told you, he has everything. My sister trails after him, hoping that he will notice her. He must laugh at her. Her pride is gone. And I would like to know why he has been here twice since you arrived.' He banged the chair arm with his fist. 'This house belongs to us. He may rule his own place, but not this. When he insisted on bringing your baggage in, my temper broke.' He fell silent as if brooding upon the memory.

Suddenly he turned his head to look straight at her. 'I could have brought your baggage in for you,' he said aggrievedly, 'and brought it from the coach if you had but mentioned it.' He continued to stare at her, waiting for her to reply.

'I – I did not think for a moment that I

would see my belongings again, John. Otherwise I would most certainly have asked you if you would fetch them.'

Suddenly it struck her that he was jealous. Had that been the main reason behind his attack on Roger? His next words made her almost certain of it.

'I saw the way he looked at you. Does he hold sway over you so soon?'

'No, that he does not,' she retorted. 'I hardly know him, though he seems pleasant enough.' She hoped that her denial sounded convincing. It was almost the truth. Roger had little, if any, influence over her. But he had aroused something more than interest in her, and she hoped very much to see him again.

John looked away at the fire, as if considering what she had said, and Ruperta added, rather unwisely: 'I know that you dislike him, but have you any good reason? Have you ever thought that he could be lonely? Perhaps his position is not the enviable one that you might think. From the little he said to me, I suspect that he is sorry that you regard him as an enemy. I am sure he would be glad if you were friends again.'

John snorted. 'He said that, did he?'

Ruperta sighed inwardly. It was no good.

She shrugged, leaned back in her chair. 'He implied as much.'

John once more transferred his gaze to the fire, but it became obvious to Ruperta that he had something on his mind, and that their conversation was not yet at an end. Whatever the subject might be, he was having trouble broaching it. At last, with an awkward movement, he turned towards her. 'I suppose that you will be leaving here soon?' All the anger and bitterness had drained from his face – only anxiety remained.

She nodded. 'I must. I have stayed only because I wished to help in return for the kindness I have received here.'

Somehow his face had become younger, boyish, though the anxiety lingered. When he spoke, it was with a shy eagerness. 'Ruperta, would you consider marrying me?'

She stared at him in utter astonishment, and was thankful when he carried on speaking, giving her time to think of some sensible reply. On a day of shocks and surprises, this was perhaps the greatest.

'You see me poor now,' he said, 'but I work hard. I have hopes that the future may be very different from the present.'

She could not possibly tell him the truth, but she must be careful in answering. It was important that John should not even guess at her feelings for Roger...

'Perhaps you think that I have behaved badly. Is that the reason why you say nothing, Ruperta?' John said when the silence between them had grown unbearable.

'I am overcome for the moment,' she murmured, gazing down into her lap. 'I thank you for the honour you have done me, but I am betrothed to a gentleman in London.'

Deep disappointment showed in her companion's face at this, and Ruperta said hastily: 'But although I have been here only a short while, I have come to regard you as a brother.' Which was the truth – a half-brother at least.

'I should have guessed. Living in London, you will meet a lot of men,' John said.

She nodded, glad that he had accepted her explanation, but was surprised when a grim smile touched his face. 'Greatly sorry as I am about your refusal of me,' he said, 'yet I am glad that Sudworth has not claimed you.'

Ruperta felt a tinge of alarm. Suppose John saw her going to Sudworth Hall with Roger...

That night Ruperta closed her bedroom door after her with a sigh of relief and tiredness. What a day it had been!

She got into bed, drifted into a half sleep. Incidents of the day returned. Roger Sudworth revealed as the highwayman. The attack on him. Jane's expression – John's proposal. And the time Roger had kissed her. She stirred restlessly at the memory, and her face grew hot in the darkness. She must be falling in love with the man…

She had been asleep for some time when a slight sound awakened her. Ruperta's eyes widened. What was it? She lifted her head to listen. The sound came again a few seconds later, at the window. She turned towards it, staring and waiting. Something hit the glass, a sharp sound in the stillness of the night.

She eased herself out of bed, and moved cautiously to the window, rubbed the panes to see more clearly. Almost directly below, the blur of a face looked up and a hand waved. What appeared to be a scarf covered most of the face. It was Roger, and as she had asked him to, he was letting her know that he was safe. She waved madly in relief, blew him a kiss, planted it against the window. Probably he could not see, but it was there from her to him. His dark figure moved away from the house, but she remained, straining her eyes to see him long after he had vanished into the surrounding night.

She slipped into bed, deeply thankful that he was safe. But what about the next night, and the one after that? How long would it be before he was caught? Ruperta shivered. When she saw him on Friday, she would try again to dissuade him from further reckless exploits...

The first half of the next day passed uneventfully. John insisted on riding out to tend his sheep, even though his injured arm was in a sling and was giving him quite a lot of pain. He seemed glad to get away from the house, Ruperta thought, or perhaps he felt awkward in her presence after what had passed between them on the previous day.

As the afternoon wore on, Ruperta became uneasy. At the back of her mind was the knowledge that Roger was to stop a coach going from Chodbury to Kinnerton. He had said that important personages were to travel in it. Then, over supper, her anxiety was increased by the news imparted by John that a certain Ned Keslett had been hanged that day on Shorrocks Moor for robbery on the highway. John explained that he had met someone from Chodbury who had told him.

Ruperta looked up from her food to catch

Jane's venomous glance. Did Jane think she had been responsible for the apprehending of that poor wretch? Had not John said his sister believed Ruperta to be an informer?

The daylight had now faded, and Ruperta's anxieties took such a hold of her that she excused herself, saying that she had a headache, and sought the solitude of her bedroom. She stared out of the window, trying to pierce the gathering mist, and praying that the coach would not set out or that Roger would have second thoughts about stopping it. Only now did she realise the strength of the rising tide of her love for him.

At every sound near the window she would leap to it, forehead pressed close against the cold panes, searching for a glimpse of the face that would tell her all was well.

Becoming tired and cold, she sat on her bed facing the window. She heard the family retiring, and her mother halted outside her door to wish her good night and hope that her headache was better.

All fell silent again, but the signal she hoped for did not come. Had he forgotten? Had he not gone out after all? Perhaps she had dozed off and missed him?

She waited and waited until her eyes would stay open no longer...

Morning came, and with it an increase in her fears regarding Roger. She even felt some anger towards him. Surely he could have kept his word and not left her to worry! But of course if he had not stopped a coach last night, then naturally he would have had no reason to come. That was it, she told herself. She had worried about nothing.

Noon found Ruperta and her mother in the parlour talking to Sir Peter. He had not gone for his usual stroll that morning, for he had developed a cough, and thought it more sensible to keep warm by the fire.

Suddenly the sound of a hard-ridden horse approaching made them look out of the windows.

'It's Jeremy!' exclaimed Mrs Colston in puzzled surprise, going to the parlour door and opening it. Ruperta heard steps along the hall, and then he came in.

'You are home early,' said his wife. 'Are you ill, Jeremy?' She was searching his face.

He waved his wife's inquiry away in great agitation. 'I am well, Ann. I am not staying, I must get back. It's Roger,' he said breathlessly. 'He did not return last night. Someone rode up from Chodbury this morning to say Roger had been caught on the Kinnerton road – holding up the coach. He's in gaol at Chodbury.'

The words pounded into Ruperta's brain. Her lips repeated them soundlessly. Roger. Caught! With a sigh she crumpled to the parlour floor…

When she came round, it was to find the others bent over her anxiously.

'I am sorry,' she said. 'It must have been the hanging yesterday, and this news now.'

The two men nodded; her mother gazed at her with deep understanding.

Ruperta was startled. Had her feelings for Roger been so noticeable? She slumped back in the chair where they had placed her. What should she do? What could she do now? He had been caught. Caught. The smiling, confident, carefree Roger.

A few minutes later, Mr Colston left to return to Sudworth Hall, and Sir Peter wandered off to fetch the book he was reading.

As soon as he had gone, Ruperta said: 'You guessed?'

The old woman nodded. 'You cannot hide feelings of that nature.'

Ruperta's expression as she looked at her mother was anguished and despairing. 'My heart became entangled. I had no wish at first that it should.' She fluttered her hands in a helpless gesture. 'Oh, what can I do?'

Her mother turned away. 'I do not know. Whatever possessed him? He had no need– I cannot believe…' She covered her face with her hands. 'Why, it is but months, it seems, since he was a boy. Laughing, roguish eyes, but the only thing he stole was my baking.' Suddenly she looked straight at Ruperta. 'They have the wrong man,' she said firmly. 'I am sure. He would not have done it.'

Something about the unchanging look of abject misery on Ruperta's face brought sudden, wide-eyed realisation. 'You believe he did it?' Ann gasped.

'He told me he was going to. I tried to dissuade him,' Ruperta whispered.

Ann stared at her. 'But why?'

Ruperta gave a laugh which was little short of hysterical. 'A challenge, he said. But he must have had another reason.' She glanced up, eyes still dulled with shock. 'What will happen to him?'

'It depends. I know little. He has not murdered, but that may not save him.'

'They hanged the last highwayman,' Ruperta said hoarsely.

The same thought had been in Ann's mind…

Later, after she had recovered from her faint, Ruperta wandered in a daze about the house. She could not keep still or settle to any work. The worst had happened. The thing she had dreaded.

She sat on the edge of her bed, utterly miserable. They had known each other for such a short time – a few hours all told. Now he was gone, knowing nothing of her feelings for him. Whether he would have returned them was another matter. It was likely that she would never find out now. She stopped crying. Was she going to crouch here snivelling while his remaining days flew by? She must think.

Just then she heard a horse's hoofs. She hurried to the window. John had returned. Perhaps he could suggest something.

She hurried downstairs and met him as he entered the hall. Perhaps he would guess at her feelings for Roger now. But that did not matter now. Nothing mattered save Roger.

'John,' she gasped, 'they've caught Roger Sudworth. Your father told us. What can be done?'

John's face puckered as if he could not understand. 'Caught, you say?'

'He's in gaol – Chodbury.'

He laughed in disbelief. 'Why?'

'R-robbed a coach. On the road to Kinnerton,' Ruperta told him.

'Sudworth!' John could not believe it.

'Please, John,' she pleaded in anguished impatience, 'what can we do to help?'

John began to smile. Then he gave a short, explosive laugh, a gleam of satisfaction in his eyes. Ruperta could hardly believe her senses.

'That is the rarest joke I've heard of.' He laughed again. 'What can we do? Do I care? What need had he to be on the road? Has he not enough money? It's greed, nothing more, I tell you.' John glanced across the hall, lowered his voice, and went on vehemently: 'He's not like me – I need money – he does not. But he must have everything, our Master Sudworth. Now he will see what is to be among the lowly.'

Shocked by his words and manner, Ruperta could only stare at her half-brother, sick at heart.

'I wonder what your London gentleman would say if he knew of your interest in Sudworth,' John said.

For Ruperta this was the last straw. She rounded on him in a fury, her eyes fierce and flashing. 'You set your horse at a defenceless man – who wants to be your friend. Roger picked you up like a baby and carried you in here, anxious that you should be better

129

quickly. Yet you laugh and say that it serves him right when I ask you to help him.'

Ruperta was conscious of figures at the kitchen and parlour doors, but she did not care. 'Has your petty pride overcome any feeling you may have had for the man who was once your play-fellow?' She choked with emotion. 'You stand with a look of satisfaction on your face. How can you? Your shame, I hope, will live with you for ever.'

Then, picking up her skirts, she dashed up the stairs, and burst into tears...

Ten minutes later she was galloping away in the direction of Chodbury, having taken one of the horses in the stable, without asking anyone's permission.

The wind rushed past, carrying away each outrageous idea for Roger's rescue as soon as it was thought of. She must do something, he could not be allowed to languish in captivity until he was hanged. Her distraught mind clutched at any solace. It may all be a mistake – it may not be Roger at all, she thought. But a cold and logical voice inside her said that it was more than likely that it was he.

Some two hours later she arrived in Chodbury. Its main street was thronged with people though the afternoon was cold and raw. A pall of smoke from many chimneys drifted slowly over the street, appearing to bring the grey sky lower.

She dismounted, seeing a small crowd of people gathered at the front of a building farther up the right hand side of the street. There seemed to be a general drift of people in that direction. She joined them, after leaving her horse at the first inn she saw.

Ruperta's heart was thumping with fear. Her mouth was dry as she asked a man next to her what was happening.

'You've not heard?' His tone expressed surprise. 'They're going in to gaze at the "golden one". Got 'im at last, so 'tis said.'

'Golden one' – Roger's gold hair. She fought to calm herself, and shuffled along with others. Beyond the doorway the light was dim. She felt cold, pulled her hood tight around her face.

'A coin, please,' said a harsh voice. She turned eyes like those of a sleepwalker upon the speaker, who had a bag held out in front of him. 'Not so soon will you see the likes of 'im again. Clever as a fox. Must 'ave bin to keep clear so long.'

Ruperta groped in her cloak pocket, and handed the gaoler a coin. Then she moved on behind the noisy column, the wall torches brightening the gloomy interior beyond.

Suddenly the entrance widened to show a cell with thick bars. There were people pushing from behind, thrusting her forward. She could not see over the heads of those in front, even when she stood on tiptoe.

Those at the back began calling for those nearer to make room and allow them to gaze on the prisoner. There was a general movement forward, and Ruperta was carried along by it until she had reached those at the very front clustered round the cell. She pushed her way between them, and her legs almost gave way under the shock of the sight before her. Her proud gallant Roger, sat humbled, his fair hair tumbled about his face. His black cloak was clutched around him.

Someone was saying: 'Always a gentleman. So handsome a man! 'Tis said he danced with one of the ladies he robbed.'

Then a voice that chilled Ruperta. 'He'll be dancing by himself afore long – on a rope. Chodbury's doing well. One highwayman gone and one to go.'

She shuddered and tried to think. She must work her way around until she was facing him. Let him see that he was not alone, try to give him some hope. But he needed something more, Ruperta realised. A miracle at the least.

Hardly aware of anything but the wish that he should see her, she worked her way along until she was in front of him, her forehead against the iron, wetting the metal with her tears. She wanted to scream out to those surrounding her to go away and leave her and the man on the other side of the bars alone. He was not an animal, a bear or a monkey, to be gazed upon.

Roger looked up, straight into Ruperta's face. She drew in her breath sharply as she saw his utter surprise, and then a sudden return of vitality and joy flashed from his blue eyes as he realised that she was really there in front of him.

'Roger,' she whispered. Now that she could actually talk to him, she was wondering what they could say to each other in front of such a large audience.

She was unprepared for what happened next. Boldly, Roger pointed at her, addressed the onlookers. 'Now here's a pretty woman! What a sight for my poor eyes to see such beauty – a change from looking at these gaolers of mine!' He sighed. 'I must confess that now I see her, I regret being in here. Why did I not meet her before?'

Ruperta stared at him in amazement. He was behaving as if he did not know her. Had the strain touched his mind?

Roger continued to address his audience, occasionally glancing at her. 'No doubt such beauty is spoken for or married to some good-for-nothing who doesn't appreciate her. I would, if I were out of here.' He shook his head, his expression one of mocking regret. 'That fellow whatever his name, is a lucky man.' He paused and regarded Ruperta intently. After a few moments he addressed her again directly and more quietly. 'I should have loved you, never mind any John, or any other man making eyes at you.'

She gave the slightest of nods. Did he mean John Colston? Was he trying to tell her something regarding him?

Roger went on: 'I would have married you straight off – no waiting. I tell you! And perhaps we would have had a son. John – I like the name. Good and honest.' He smiled ruefully. 'I fear that is all a dream – but perhaps you will not deny me a kiss.'

All eyes were turned on them as Roger came forward and clutched two of the cell bars. They kissed each other.

How different from their last kiss, private

and quiet in the shelter of the woods on the way back to the house! Her lips trembled against his.

'Under the tree, all to John,' he murmured, and it took her a few moments to realise that he was talking of his buried hoard.

'There!' he addressed the onlookers with a flourish of his hand. 'I shall take that memory with me.' He glanced at Ruperta again. 'You must come to my farewell party – the date has not yet been decided.'

In abject misery and hopelessness, Ruperta just stood there, her mind in a turmoil of emotions. He must not talk like that! She was conscious of a woman's voice near by.

'Pity if he hangs, he'd be more use to me than my Jack. A right, proper man!'

The gaoler spoke up. 'He's not to hang.' He paused and Ruperta swung towards him, clutching at a hope. 'Not yet awhile, anyways,' he went on.

Ruperta fought for control of herself, to appear an unconcerned spectator. 'How long will he be here?' she asked, unable to stifle the trembling in her voice.

He looked at her coldly. Another lovelorn one – yearning for a handsome man behind bars. He'd seen it before. 'He'll be tried in a day or two. When Sir George Ely returns. A stern judge he is.'

His shrug and ensuing silence were eloquent enough for her to guess the rest.

She stayed until she was told to leave, having stood numb and miserable. It was too late for their love to flower...

She left Chodbury in the dusk, heedless of possible dangers, her tears borne away by uncaring wind. Her mind was full of the man she had left behind. What could she do? One woman against the law of the land.

All to John, he had said. He wanted his secret hoard to go to one whom he still counted as a friend – a man who had tried to harm him. A man who ought to be relied on for immediate help, but who had turned away. Ruperta raged against John during her lonely ride. She realised now that Roger had turned highwayman to help John and his family.

Ruperta shivered uncontrollably. Roger, having abandoned all hope for himself, was intent on helping a man who now, it appeared, cared nothing for him. She could not bring herself to accept that his death was inevitable, and would not tell John what Roger had said about his having the buried hoard. It was too final. Some way must be found to save Roger.

On returning to Ravall's Court, Ruperta had not wanted to face anyone, but in deference to her mother's wish had gone in to supper. There she had poked and prodded at her food, and answered with difficulty the eager questions put to her about her visit to Chodbury.

The inquiries came mainly from her mother, Mr Colston and Sir Peter. John avoided her eyes, but she cared little for that – no help was forthcoming from that quarter, that had been made clear earlier in the day. As for Jane, half-way through the meal she suddenly shoved her plate away, got up and left the kitchen.

For a while, after supper, Ruperta sat in the parlour with the family. There was some discussion of what might be done to help Roger, but the Colstons and Sir Peter had little money or influence, and it was not likely that they would be able to do very much. Still, they would try.

John sat at a corner, occasionally joining in, but for the most part silent and sunk into himself. And Jane sat a little behind Ruperta in the shadows, making her feel most uncomfortable by her silent hostility.

Ruperta was glad to get away to her

bedroom, to try and find a solution to the problem of freeing the man she loved. A brooding silence lay upon the house and its occupants – all, it seemed, busy with their own thoughts regarding the capture and imprisonment of Roger Sudworth.

Ruperta got into bed, lay awake thinking of him in captivity, and with so little hope. If only she could hear a stone against the window, look down and see him wave as he had done the night before he was caught…

She must have drifted off into sleep, awakening to the feel of cool air upon her face. She listened, but the night was silent.

She lay back again, memory returning with thoughts of Roger. She would go again to visit him the next day, and the next, until…

Ruperta's eyes, accustomed to the darkness, now became aware of a blacker patch in front of her. Suddenly it moved nearer, filling the space in front of her. With a shock that nearly stopped her heart, she realised that someone was there standing over her.

Hardly breathing, Ruperta began to lift her head very slowly upwards. Her eyes travelled up the black column of the intruder's body. Glimpsed the pale blur of the hands, the face above.

'I could not sleep,' Jane's voice was sullen.

'And you – you slept like a baby. In spite of all the harm you have done since you came here. Not content with being an informer, you have to take Roger away from me.'

She grasped Ruperta's wrist and twisted it so that she screamed. The sound seemed to being Jane to her senses.

'If Mother hears that, she'll be in to see what the matter is,' she said sourly. 'I had better go.'

She slipped out. Ruperta shut the door after her, then sank on to her bed, shaking. She wished most heartily that she had left the house after her first night there. She had seen her mother, that was what she had come for. That should have been all. Instead she had stayed on, to become involved in the Colstons' affairs. Now she could not leave the district because of Roger.

There was a knock on her door. She heard her mother's voice asking if all was well. Ruperta sighed heavily in the darkness. No, it was not, but she welcomed the inquiry, opened the door and let her mother in.

'I heard a scream, Ruperta,' Ann Colston said.

'A dream, a nightmare, Mother,' the girl said, forcing herself to sound calm.

'I have been praying,' said Ann, 'for

Roger's freedom and your happiness. I could not sleep.'

Ruperta said softly: 'I have come all this way and found you, for which I am thankful. And I have found a man to love.' Her voice broke. 'Yet he is taken from me. It is the end before the beginning.'

Mrs Colston patted her daughter's face tenderly. 'There may yet be something, dear Ruperta, that can be done,' she murmured. But both knew that it was only a matter of time before he would be put to death.

Soon afterwards her mother left, and Ruperta bolted the door after her in case Jane should decide to return. Then she went back to bed, and the next thing she knew the sunlight was flooding the room.

She got up and dressed. Her mirror showed her pale and haggard.

She thought of her decision to visit Roger again. She must get there early. She tried to think of something positive to help him. Perhaps she might hear that a measure of leniency would be extended to him. Whatever was to happen, she must go, she must not fail him now.

Going downstairs she thought that perhaps John would accompany her to Chodbury, though after the way she had spoken to him it was unlikely. Joining her mother and Sir Peter in the kitchen she learned that John had gone out. Well, what had she expected? He would not take action for the sake of a man he now detested.

Ruperta ate a small and hurried breakfast, and informed the others of her plan to visit Roger again. Both expressed great concern, and tried to dissuade her from going, but she was politely adamant that she must.

At this Sir Peter offered to accompany her. 'I may be old, but I would be better than no escort at all,' he said.

Half an hour later they set out, Ruperta feeling more secure at having the companionship of Sir Peter. But the brightness of the day did nothing to raise her spirits, and such conversation as there was came mainly from him. She did notice, however, that he seemed less aged and more erect in the saddle than he appeared in his chair or around the house.

At one stage, after several silent and thoughtful minutes, he said: 'I cannot understand young Roger Sudworth being involved in highway robbery. He was an honest youngster, something of a daredevil at times. Once he nearly got himself killed.'

Ruperta, only half listening, and eager to

reach Chodbury, now looked at her companion with more interest.

He glanced at her, perhaps pleased to have aroused her curiosity. 'He and John were young boys then, of eleven or twelve – I forget. They went swimming from the beach at the back of the house. You know where it is?'

She nodded. 'Yes, I've walked down there.'

'Roger swam out to some rocks,' continued Sir Peter, 'and as time means nothing to boys, forgot about the tide. He tried to return but got into difficulties. I'm not sure just what happened, but John brought him ashore, though he owned that he did not know how he had done it. Anyway, he saved Roger's life, and Roger never forgot that.' Sir Peter sighed. 'And to think that there has been bad blood between them these last years!'

Was that another reason for Roger's attempt to help John financially? Perhaps, Ruperta thought, Roger felt he had a debt to repay.

She turned to the old man. 'From what I have heard, sir,' she said, 'it appears that John is envious of his former friend.'

Sir Peter looked at her ruefully. 'It has not taken you long to notice that aspect of Colston family life. You are quite right,

142

though I wish that it was not so. I sit in my chair and I hear things, see expressions. My daughter does not tell me everything, but I think and wonder.' Suddenly his tone became brisk. 'But whatever is wrong between the two, I cannot believe that Roger is guilty of highway robbery. I think it is a case of mistaken identity – I shall plead at the trial for him. There is a chance that he will be acquitted, I feel sure.'

Ruperta said nothing. Roger was guilty. She had nothing to cling to – no hope. He had been caught.

Sir Peter gave her an uncomfortably shrewd glance and said: 'Let us hasten. We must see what state the poor fellow's in.'

They found that there was no crowd outside the building. It was still early in the day – earlier than when Ruperta had come the day before. With Sir Peter she made straight for a place as near Roger as possible. He was gazing out at those present with a thoughtful air. The hunted, despondent look of yesterday had gone.

Suddenly he saw her, and his face flooded with delight, his eyes danced as if twin candles had appeared behind them. With an air of authority he pointed at those in front of Ruperta. 'Make way, make way! Allow

143

this lady through. She came yesterday to see me. I must have her favour. Come, stand before me.'

The people parted and she stood face to face with him again, Sir Peter behind and forgotten. 'Good morning, mistress,' Roger said. 'Your pretty face is becoming known to me. I thank you for coming.'

She noticed that his eyes were grave, though he was still smiling easily. He went on, speaking very quietly: 'I want you to marry me – I shall die a happy man, and you will be provided for. Later, you can marry any John, Tom or Jack you desire. Now, what say you to that?'

He was proposing that she should have the Hall, and also indirectly giving John the chance to obtain what he had coveted. Had Roger offered her marriage when he was a free man, she would have been blissfully happy. But the proposal with the bars of the cell between them, and Roger resigned to his death, plunged her into despair.

People pressed closer. Eyes fastened on them, and there were murmurs of sympathy and encouragement.

Ruperta determined that she would not let him down. She forced herself to speak lightly and gaily. 'Marry you? Yes, but not because of your possessions.' Her voice faltered as she went on, pretence vanishing and her real emotion revealed for all to hear. 'You yourself would be all that I wanted.'

Applause and noises of approval came from those gathered around.

She turned away, choked with emotion. She had meant what she had said, but could not play the terrible game any longer.

'My heart is full of joy. I thank you,' Roger said.

She could not trust herself to look back at him. If she was going to help him, she must try and keep alert, to grasp at anything that offered hope for him.

Sir Peter was talking to a gaoler, and Ruperta decided that she would wait until he had finished his conversation, because in her distraught state she was quite likely to say something that would incriminate Roger even further.

A minute later she saw that Sir Peter's conversation had ended and she approached him hurriedly. 'If you agree, sir, I should like to go home now, please.'

Sir Peter looked at the young woman with great compassion. Roger had indeed woven his charms about her heart. And that was a pity. It seemed to him that it was a foregone conclusion that Roger would not live long enough to bring her happiness.

Just as they were leaving, Ruperta glanced back. Roger was sitting there, calm and impassive. It was as if their public conversation had never been, but there was some comfort in the fact that they had proclaimed their love for each other.

When they mounted, she asked Sir Peter: 'What is the news, sir? Have they named the day of the trial?'

'Tomorrow, at eleven. Sir George Ely will preside.'

'Tomorrow, at eleven! Sir George Ely,' she repeated numbly.

'Yes,' said Sir Peter. 'He is no better, no worse than any other judge.'

'This Sir George – will he journey overnight?'

Sir Peter seemed mildly surprised, looking at her curiously before answering: 'He has not far to come. He lives at Foxholme.' He gestured to his right. 'Across the moor – there lies the road.'

'Shorrocks Moor.' There was a catch in her voice. The gallows stood on the moor.

Sir Peter turned to her, his expression puzzled and reflective. 'It's very strange. I have known Roger since he was a child, yet he chose not to recognise me today. He could not have failed to see me. And he needs friends now.'

'Perhaps it was so that he did not bring dishonour to anyone he knew well,' she suggested.

'If that is the case,' said Sir Peter, 'I thank him for it, but there was no need. Oh, why did the young fool see himself as a gentleman of the road? First time out, I'll wager – and he's caught.'

Ruperta was now too tired and miserable to correct him even if she had wanted to.

Sir Peter drew nearer, gave her a comforting pat on her shoulder. 'I am sorry that your visit to us has been so troubled. I have observed your feelings for young Sudworth. But try not to think too much about tomorrow. New hope comes with the new day.'

To which Ruperta nodded, and managed a smile of thanks for his encouragement, but her hopes were fading.

CHAPTER SIX

Ruperta was very near despair. Her second visit to Roger had provided no answer to the problem of how to help him. And there was so little time.

Could her father help? But he was with the Court at Salisbury or with Kings Charles at Wilton House. He might even be with the Fleet, preparing for war. Even if a message could reach him in time, she guessed that it was hardly likely that he would intercede for a common highway thief, though it would be for her sake...

Her mind darted here and there. Sir George Ely. Could she not appeal to him in person? She dismissed the idea immediately. Had not Sir Peter said that Sir George was no better and no worse than others in his attitude to captured highwaymen? No, any appeal that she made on Roger's behalf would have to be at the trial itself.

In the darkness she saw again the image of his face behind the bars of that cell, and forced herself to think of his bizarre proposal of marriage to her.

If she married him, she would, if the trial went against him, be a beneficiary under his Will. And John, Roger thought, would also benefit, for he believed that John and Ruperta would marry. Ruperta wished that she had been able to tell Roger why such a marriage could not possibly take place.

She wanted him, not his property or money. Just him alone, looking at her with those devil-may-care blue eyes. But the hand of love had been held out only to be snatched away from her for ever. She broke down and wept bitterly.

Later, when she had recovered, she joined the family downstairs for a short while, and found that Sir Peter had acquainted them with every detail of his and Ruperta's visit to Chodbury. All but John were going to attend the trial. It seemed that he was still nursing his grievance against Roger. Ruperta shrugged mentally. It was of no consequence now.

She told the Colstons that she could not face the strain of the trial after her two visits to Roger. This was perfectly true, but it also served to give her time to do something to help him. Feverishly her mind ran over the courses she might take...

By the time she went up to her room she was resolved on what she had to do the next day to try and save Roger. There would be no turning back from her plan. Tomorrow was going to be the most momentous and dangerous day of her life so far.

She was up before dawn, having slept fitfully, impatiently awaiting the departure of her mother and Mr Colston, Sir Peter and Jane. It was a subdued party that set out for Chodbury, the sadness and tension of the occasion having its effect on all, and the open antagonism of Jane towards Ruperta had further upset Ann.

Ruperta felt sorry for her mother, but that morning had very little emotion left to spend on any other than Roger Sudworth. She had so much to accomplish in the few hours before the trial began.

Once the three Colstons and Sir Peter had departed, Ruperta hurried back inside the house and went from room to room downstairs. Where was John? She must know. He was not to be found. She went upstairs and, glancing from the gallery window, saw him mounting his horse. She stood back and watched him ride away. Now she must hasten.

She made for John's room. A pair of boots

151

lay in a corner. She grabbed them, and snatched up a hat. Then she rushed back to her own room, afraid that John might return to the house again.

For a moment she stood against her door, trembling with the thought of what was to come next. Then she went downstairs, dashed into the parlour, snatched the pistol from the wall above the fire-place.

Ten minutes later she was galloping away from the house, in the direction she had taken with Roger Sudworth on the day he had returned her ring to her. She wore John's boots, and her skirts were hitched up so that she could ride astride. Inside her cloak was jammed his hat, and the gun felt heavy against her side.

The day had now revealed its intentions fully. It was dank, misty and cold. It was weather well suited to a trial, but also to the task she had to do…

The far edge of the wood was now visible, and the darker strip of highway beyond. Across it there was more woodland. No wonder it had often been the scene of the holding up of coaches, for it afforded shelter and a way of escape. It was somewhere near by that Roger had stopped the coach she had been travelling in.

Reaching the edge of the wood Ruperta now turned right, following the highway, but keeping to its side and near the wood. She rode on, searching ahead for signs of another road joining the one she was following. Was she wrong? Was it possible she was not on the Chodbury road? The thought of what that might mean to her chance of saving Roger drove her frantic. It must be farther on. Shorrocks Moor suggested an open space, whereas she was surrounded by woodland.

She became conscious of a sound ahead – a metallic one, like the jingling of coins. She stopped, strained to hear. It came again, though it seemed no nearer. Was it a coach? Sir George's? She urged the horse on, moving quietly on the grass. The chinking sound grew louder.

Through the thickening mist she saw the trees to her left ended about a hundred yards farther on with grey space beyond. Was that the beginning of Shorrocks Moor? She rode faster, her eyes searching the ground ahead in acute anxiety for signs of another road joining the one she was on.

The sound came again, and now she could see the cause of it. She clung with horror and shock to her horse's neck trying to ward off the sight in front of her. Black against the grey the gallows stood out. There was a man hanging in chains from it.

It must be Ned Keslett, who had been hanged a few days ago. Horror gripped her, and for a moment she almost forgot why she was there.

Perhaps it was the horse, impatient to be moving again, that aroused her from her shocked state. Minutes were going by. Precious minutes. She must do what she had set out to do, otherwise the next figure swinging in chains would be Roger's. She shuddered, forced herself to pass the gallows, fixing her thoughts on finding the road along which Sir George would travel.

Within a matter of yards she had found a narrow road to the left stretching into the mist. But was that the one she was looking for? Why had she not got every detail, however small, from Sir Peter?

She could go on and wait, but in that case she might stop the wrong coach. She would be risking her life with no benefit to Roger.

Deciding to wait there, she moved off into the gloom and shelter of the trees opposite to where the two roads met. From under her cloak she tugged John's hat and put it on, and from her pocket she brought a kerchief, which she tied across her face. Then she lined up her horse behind a great tree and waited, now and again touching the metal of the pistol in her pocket.

Doubts now assailed her. What was the hour? Sir George could have left early, or stayed in Chodbury overnight. If he came, what was she going to do? Plead at the roadside with him? Voices of laughing mockery seemed to echo from the trees around...

Her eyes strayed to the gallows just visible between the trees up the road. That could be her fate for what she was about to do. What was she doing here in any case? She had stepped right outside her settled, ordered life. Now here she was on the King's Highway, mounted and armed, about to commit a crime which carried the death penalty. And all for what?

She pulled the pistol from her pocket, and found it difficult to keep her hand steady. She felt sick. Her inner being screamed at her to race away. To change her mind and attend the trial. Make an impassioned plea for Roger. Ask for a delay, and hope that if she secured a breathing space she could get her father to use his influence. Anything but this, this terrible madness which had taken hold of her and was forcing her to become a criminal. Not for monetary gain, but because of her love for the man whose trial was to begin that very morning.

Her horse's head lifted, ears pricked to indicate the approach of its own kind. She leaned forward, straining to see.

A coach came into view, two horses pulling it. It was fifty yards away and there appeared to be no escort. She must catch it head on.

She gave a sob of agonised indecision, staring as if in a trance as the green and black carriage approached. Twenty-five yards to the turn. Was it Sir George Ely's coach? And now may heaven help me, she thought, and rode out of the wood.

'Stop – hold!' Her voice was unsteady, but the driver brought the coach to a halt almost at the junction of the roads. 'Get down.' She tried to lower her voice, and displayed the pistol. The driver clambered down, looking sullen.

She took a deep breath and shouted: 'Who rides in there?'

An irate voice came from inside the carriage. 'What have you stopped for?' Then a head peered from its interior. There was a dead silence as the man took in the sight of the coachman on the ground and the menacing figure beyond him.

Ruperta moved forward until she was almost abreast of the carriage door. She glimpse a woman behind the man. 'Come out. I must know who you are.' She had difficulty in trying to disguise her voice.

The door opened, and a stiff, well dressed man got out, his eyes smouldering, brown and angry. He studied Ruperta carefully, noting and memorising.

'I am Sir George Ely. You will have cause to remember that in the near future,' he said harshly.

The man she wanted! Her mind raced. She nodded at the woman, and indicated that she was to get out of the coach. The fair, nervous little creature obeyed.

'And who is this?' Ruperta demanded.

'My wife,' Sir George said curtly. 'If you rob us, I'll make sure that our property is returned. And you will be punished.'

Affecting a resolution she did not possess, Ruperta ordered the woman to approach.

Sir George's wife glanced at her husband, then came forward and halted a yard in front of Ruperta's horse. Ruperta kept the pistol pointed at her. A woman captive would be easier to manage than a man.

Ruperta said to Sir George: 'An exchange. Roger Sudworth – the man you were to try this morning – for the return of your wife. Bring him here in an hour's time. Otherwise it will be the worse for her.'

For a moment Ruperta thought that she had lost and that Sir George was going to take a chance, but his wife's muttered, frightened plea to him made him turn for his carriage. Once inside he put his head out, and said: 'By the sound of you you're young, but I'll make sure you don't grow much older.' He pointed towards the gallows. 'There's room for two more there,' he flung at her fiercely.

Ruperta watched as the coach turned into the Chodbury road and set off at a swift pace. When it had disappeared from sight she led Sir George's wife a short distance into the wood. Lady Ely was upset and frightened, wondering what was going to happen to her, and Ruperta had some sympathy for her – she herself had suffered in much the same way not so long ago. She wished she could say something reassuring to the captive, but did not dare for fear of being recognised as a woman.

She dismounted and sank on to a log from which she had a clear view of the road. Truth to tell, her legs would not have supported her for much longer. The strain of the hold-up had left her trembling and weak.

Would they really bring Roger and exchange him for Lady Ely? And if they did, would escape be possible? Problems she had never envisaged before now presented themselves. Sir George might bring soldiers and surround the place...

She glanced at Sir George's wife. Why not just leave here and escape? So simple – so easy. To go home and forget. But a voice inside her shouted against such cowardice. She must carry out her plan. It was Roger's only chance.

How long had Sir George been gone? At every movement of twig or leaf or rustle in the undergrowth, Ruperta went cold, looking around her in stark terror. If only it were a play nearing its end, when the masks could be flung off, and the actors applauded. But it was all too real.

Her horse snorted, pawed the ground impatiently, looked back past her. Ruperta turned. A horseman was approaching them slowly from inside the wood. Then the trees seemed to waver, as in her stupefied amazement she recognised the face. It was John!

She hurried over to him unsteadily, at the same time slipping her kerchief down from her face. If Sir George's wife heard names, it could be highly dangerous.

It was some time before John found his tongue. At last he said: 'I was curious, so I followed you...' He looked beyond her to the woman huddled on the ground, her back to them. Slowly he dismounted.

In a low voice Ruperta told him what she had done, and saw admiration joined by growing apprehension on her half-brother's features.

'Shield your face,' hissed Ruperta. 'And be off – you need not share my danger.'

'No! For the sake of our old friendship I cannot fail Roger. And I must tell you that I guessed your love was for him.'

'You must think of your parents ... of the risks you run...'

'I am here – I shall stay,' retorted John.

Ruperta felt too much relieved by his presence to argue any more. She gazed own the road. It was still empty.

Suddenly she remembered something. 'But you have only one good arm,' she protested.

'It is enough. At least I shall sound like a man and, if I have to, I can shoot straight.' He looked at the pistol she held. 'Where did you get that?'

'From the parlour,' she told him.

'And you held up the coach with that?'

She nodded. He took it from her and examined it, then handed it back. 'It's not loaded – has not been fired for years. If anyone had loaded it and tried to fire it, it would probably have burst.'

Ruperta felt quite faint. She had not stopped to think whether it was loaded or not when she had snatched it from the parlour wall.

John produced a pistol from beneath his cloak. 'This one works, and for good measure I have another at my saddle.'

Ruperta's eyes flew up the road again. Still no sign. The waiting was becoming unbearable. 'Do you think that they...'

John nodded. 'Yes. We have his wife. Sir George must return with Roger.'

Ruperta had thought of something else.

'If Roger is freed, where can we hide him? He cannot go home.' She strained her eyes again into the distance, while her companion considered.

'The cave. He will be safe there,' John said.

Momentarily, her heart lifted. John was Roger's friend again.

'John, the money Roger stole was for you.

I know where it is hidden.' Then she told him about Roger's proposal of marriage; and wished she hadn't when she saw the mortification on John's face.

'My shame will give me courage to free him,' he said, staring down the road.

'He could not understand why you hated him, John. He owed you his life, and he wanted to help you.' Her thoughts raced ahead. 'When Roger is freed we must separate.'

John nodded. 'And I think we ought to mount now – we must be ready. They're not to be trusted.' He was tying a scarf over the lower part of his face as he spoke.

She watched as he remounted awkwardly. 'John, lend me one of your pistols, please.'

He handed one over. 'Do be careful. I will go to meet them and make the exchange. Better that you follow with the woman.'

Ruperta looked at him and said firmly: 'I shall go first. You see to Lady Ely.'

'No.' John shook his head. 'It is too dangerous.'

'Dangerous?' Ruperta laughed – a strained, harsh sound in the quiet of the wood. 'Did I not hold the coach up without you?' she said sharply. 'I must finish what I set out to do.'

John had nothing to say to that.

Ruperta knew her nerves were in pieces. It was all she could do to control them, waiting and not knowing what was going to happen. But she felt that as the first half of her plan had succeeded, so might the next part.

She pulled the kerchief over her face, and began to edge the horse nearer to the road. 'Bring her when I wave,' she said over her shoulder. The mist had lifted a little.

She looked back at the road and caught her breath. A coach was approaching some two hundred yards away. Green and black – yes, it was Sir George's. But now there were three horsemen besides. Two soldiers and between them a dark figure with fair hair. Roger! Her heart thudded.

She took a deep breath, urged the horse into the road, and stood facing the other party. Waved to the waiting John. Slowly, with Lady Ely between them, they advanced to halt when within about a hundred yards of the coach.

John's pistol was levelled at Sir George's wife. Her husband got down from the coach. No doubt he was surprised to see two highwaymen where there had been one before.

Ruperta wondered if her voice would

carry to him. 'Free your prisoner, Sir George, let him come. You shall receive your wife.' Her voice, to her surprise, came out stronger than she had expected. Perhaps the comfort of John by her side, and Roger almost within reach of freedom had something to do with it.

Sir George told Roger to dismount.

'No,' shouted Ruperta, 'he brings the horse with him.' If not, they would have two horses between three people. If they were going to separate, they needed a horse each.

Sir George hesitated and seemed about to refuse; then he gestured savagely at Roger, who remounted and moved forward.

Ruperta waited, very still. When Roger had covered half the distance, John sent Lady Ely forward and she, needing no further bidding, set off uttering little shrieks of relief.

When Roger had reached his friends, Ruperta unable to contain herself any longer, turned and with him fled into the woods. John followed, leaving the plump figure making for her husband and the coach.

'Separate!' shouted John hurrying after them. A shot followed him. The pursuit was on.

Ruperta tore off the kerchief and turned to

Roger. 'The cave, Roger, the cave!'

A mixture of surprise, joyous recognition and fear for her showed in his face as they looked at each other. He reached across, touched her, a smile lighting up his face. 'My love!'

She was so happy that she almost forgot the danger they were in as she spurred ahead. The other two rode off in different directions. She was alone. Must get as near to the house as possible, then wait for nightfall, she decided.

She bent and dodged overhanging branches, with the horse picking its way carefully over the rough ground. At any moment she was expecting to hear the sounds of pursuit. But she had succeeded. Roger was free...

Something glinted immediately ahead. Then dark objects bobbed up and down, coming towards her. At first her mind would not register what they were – soldiers spreading out ahead. She was twenty-five yards away before she could bring her mount to a walking pace. Icy dread clutched her.

The leader came forward. 'What is your hurry, sir? Would you be hastening from the Chodbury road?'

Ruperta found the hysteria that threatened to overwhelm her. 'H-have I not the right to ride here by myself?' She found it difficult to disguise her voice now.

'You ride as if pursued by fiends.'

'I came farther than I had intended, and am now hastening home,' she replied.

The soldier came closer. 'And where might that be?'

She must not mention Ravall's Court. How had she been so naïve as to think that other soldiers would not have been posted in the surrounding area? 'Chodbury, but I think I may have lost my way.'

He edged nearer, pistol drawn, scrutinising her closely. 'A woman!' he said, surprised.

Ruperta snatched at a last hope. 'Cannot a woman ride alone?'

'Yes, but you are strangely dressed. A man's hat! Take it off.'

Ruperta bared her head, heard the murmurs from the others.

The leader's eyes wandered over her. 'A gentlewoman riding astride, and wearing a man's boots. Open your cloak,' he ordered harshly.

With fingers that would barely act, Ruperta fumbled at the garment. The pistols were revealed.

Triumph showed on the man's face. 'Sir George said a youth held him up. We have the truth – a woman did it. This one. Take her.' He motioned to his men.

Ruperta could have argued the pistols were for her own protection. But her nerve had gone. She wheeled her horse to flee. Anywhere. The nightmare had returned. The horse stumbled and half fell, throwing her to the ground.

Rough hands pulled her to her feet and set her on the horse. Her hands were tied behind her, and one of the soldiers led her horse by the bridle...

Ruperta's capture made a great sensation. A woman had held up a coach! Something new. The crowds flocked to see her. There was a good deal of sympathy for her when the tale of how she had risked her life for love's sake became known. That she would die was a foregone conclusion, but the man was still free. The story touched the hearts of all, except perhaps Sir George who had suffered the indignity of being held up by a young woman. He was the butt of many a joke.

As for Ruperta, she was in a state of increasing terror as the hours went by. The numbing shock of the capture had gone, and the consequences of her action were hideously plain.

The rows of pale blurred faces peered and went. She thought she saw her mother once, helpless and sobbing, Jane gloating and taunting. Was that Sir Peter, shocked and grey-faced? She was too dazed to be sure.

And the man she loved, where was he? He had asked her to marry him, called her his love in their brief meeting after the rescue. She bent her head in angry bitterness. Why was there no word from him? Had she not saved him? It might be difficult for him to get word to her, but surely he could find some means of letting her know that he was doing all he could to help her?

In her desperation she implored the gaoler to let her write to Prince Rupert. She knew she would not be believed if she said that she was his daughter; but she declared that the Prince was an old friend of her family, and would come to her aid.

The gaoler roared with laughter, and said that he admired her spirit but didn't believe a word of what she had told him.

Her mother would know that the Prince could probably be found at Court, and might contrive to get a letter to him. But would it reach him in time?

Sir George was determined to make an example of Ruperta, and her trial was pushed through with indecent speed. She was found guilty and sentenced to be hanged on Shorrocks Moor the following day.

That night she slept not at all, and on the following morning went through the business of seeing a clergyman and being urged to confess. The parson found her very quiet, but obstinate. She insisted that she had done what she had to do and had harmed no one in the process. After that she would say no more.

She was led out and helped into a cart. Already a crowd had gathered to follow her to Shorrocks Moor. Sir George and various officers of the law were present, together with a small escort of soldiers.

It is doubtful if Ruperta was aware of everything going on about her. She wore her cloak over her dress, yet was chilled to the bone. The cart jerked forward, she clinging to its side, looking out on to the faces that surrounded her. People waved from the shops, leaned out of windows, as she passed. Innkeepers offered her wine or beer, and one of them told her that she could pay him on the way back.

'Don't refuse, my lovely. Take one or two,' said someone else.

The cart halted and she gulped down a glass of wine. Fear and cold made her teeth chatter, but she managed to thank the man who had brought her the drink.

They started off again, the cart swaying this way and that. Her legs trembled and would not support her, so she knelt at the front of the cart clutching the wooden rail and looking over the horse's back.

Then she saw Roger. He wore rough, homespun clothes and he was mounted on a powerful-looking horse. What did he hope to accomplish at this late stage?

They were now at the boundary of the town and, a hundred yards on, the road divided. The right-hand branch went to Shorrocks Moor, the other straight ahead to freedom. Ravall's Court, every day things. Only a few days ago she had been on that road with Sir Peter after visiting Roger. Only a few days ago…

Her mind fastened on Roger. His empty words – empty love. He had been nothing, of no substance. A shadow. All talk. He had not even tried to see her until now when it was too late. She laid her head on the jerking rail.

The movement of the cart ceased. She

raised her head slowly. Was she there already?

Ruperta was aware of the noise of the crowd around the cart, the orders of the soldiers to keep back. It was nearly the end. The final and desperate flicker of hope had gone.

She dragged herself to her feet, supporting herself on the cart front, facing forwards and shivering.

The crowd had hushed, waiting for the customary farewell speech…

Suddenly Roger's horse reared, appearing to be quite out of control. It bolted, and the crowd scattered before it. Shouting, swaying in the saddle, Roger was heading for her.

Ruperta shed her cloak, made for the side of the cart. The horse, under control again, paused briefly, and Ruperta, skirts kilted to the knee, managed to scramble up behind Roger. Her arms went round his waist, and then they were racing up the road, shouts and confusion behind them.

Roger had timed the mock bolting to perfection. A second earlier or a second later and the rescue would have been impossible. As it was, had even one man kept his head and been courageous enough to try to stop the horse, the escape attempt would certainly have failed.

Ruperta prayed that the horse would not stumble, for if it went lame they might still be caught. Then there was only one thought in her mind: Roger loved her, he had come for her, facing fearful odds to save her life. He loved her, she loved him.

For a moment Ruperta was on a solitary, summer cloud flying over sun-dappled ground...

They passed Ravall's Court and halted near the top of the path leading to the inlet. Roger was off and pulling at her hand almost before she touched the ground, and they ran down the path. Mr Colston and Sir Peter took charge of the horse, and wished the fugitives good fortune.

Ruperta heard someone call her name, glanced back. Her mother was hurrying towards her. A brief choked moment as they embraced. 'Ruperta, remember me!'

'Dearest mother!' So much to say. No time for more than the briefest of thanks from Ann to Roger; then he and Ruperta were hurrying across the shingle, hand in hand. A figure by a small boat at the water's edge. It was John. Beyond him a ship, indistinct in the sea mist.

Roger and John shook hands; Ruperta kissed John and bade him farewell.

They urged her into the boat. The men pushed off, Roger leapt in, rowed strongly away from the shore. The waving figure grew small at the water's edge, and Ruperta looked ahead at the bulk of the ship looming up before her. Willing hands pulled them aboard.

Then, heedless of those around, they fell into each other's arms. Ruperta felt quite giddy – and there were so many questions to ask. But she and Roger were safe, and together...

The ship slid slowly out to sea. And Ruperta looked up at the sails and her heart was filled with a great happiness. Now the promise of life was as full for her as it had been empty that morning.

Down below in their cabin, they engaged in excited and loving question and answer, Roger telling her how he had disguised himself and bought a horse that no one in the district would recognise, and how John had arranged the passage in the ship now taking them away, paying in advance with the money hidden in the cave.

'One day,' said Roger softly, 'we may be able to thank John properly for all he has done. But in the meantime, kiss me. I love you.'

Her lips met his in joy; then she moved her head away. One more question. 'Where are we going, Roger?'

'To the Channel Islands. Some cousins of mine live there. We'll be married, and stay with them.'

She must get word to her father, Ruperta thought. He would use his influence with his cousin, the King.

The Prince would be furious with her. But his fits of anger seldom lasted for very long. Besides, the tale of the rescue – the two rescues – would appeal to him. Daring, quick thinking and horsemanship were three of his leading characteristics and he was always ready to appreciate these qualities in others.

She glanced up, met Roger's vivid blue gaze, and gave a little sigh of pure happiness.

The publishers hope that this book has given you enjoyable reading. Large Print Books are especially designed to be as easy to see and hold as possible. If you wish a complete list of our books please ask at your local library or write directly to:

Dales Large Print Books
Magna House, Long Preston,
Skipton, North Yorkshire.
BD23 4ND

This Large Print Book, for people
who cannot read normal print,
is published under the auspices of

THE ULVERSCROFT FOUNDATION